UNFANTASTIC

A Novel

By Towns

For my family

Special thanks to Michael

His hand pressed against the damp bark of an old oak tree.
"Why?" he asked, looking up into its dying leaves.
And with the gentle breeze of late September, it replied,
without a word, "Because."

-Mia Simone

UNFANTASTIC

December 24th, 1960
Or, Becoming Me

There was color. And there was sound.

This was the final moment of a drifting life.

It was floating at the edge of its creation, gazing at a mystery through which it would travel and, consequentially, become.

He had felt subtle impressions of an ego before, passing instances in which the objects around him confusingly seemed not to exist within himself. Soon that heavy idea would stay with him until the day of his death. It would leave him only in a few fleeting moments of illumination, times when he saw the wholeness of his existence, times which to him would be the most important of his life.

His hands gripped the soft fabric wrapped around his body. His small fingers squeezed with all of their delicate strength. The warm, red vastness ahead of him burned with scattered shades of green, while drops of blue and yellow slowly flickered amongst the glow.

A deep voice that wasn't his mother's swam through the space surrounding him, though her silent scent of love drifted nearby. He remembered, without words, without meaning, without anything at all, the smell she gave to his senses as he would drink the liquid life from their body. It was theirs, not hers or his, because they were one. He came from her blood, her flesh, her innermost spaces. He grew within her mind as they shared thoughts of which neither of them were aware.

But soon her body would become solely hers.

His would be his.

And the one would become two.

The shape of someone entered the center of his vision. Familiar hands moved down and around him. They weren't the gentle hands of his mother, but they were still hands well known. Within their firm grasp he was safe. Yet, for the first time in his life he felt a hint of being painfully alone.

He couldn't understand the words being spoken to him. With the incoherent flow of sounds came a bitter smell, which unbeknownst to him arose from the mixture of whiskey, ham, and olives brewing in his father's stomach.

The world slowly spun as he was carried across the room. He and his father stopped beside a group of silhouettes standing before a brilliant white glow. Their shapes and sounds and smells were strangely pulling at his thoughts. Everything was within him, and he was within everything, yet a small rupture of divorce was being born between the two. There was self, an embryonic awareness that he was distinct, and there was other, the newly born idea that the universe outside his skin was something separate from who he was.

However, the valley being formed between his mind and the world outside was still a shallow gap. The blinding white behind the shadowed bodies was still a part of his being, and desire still led the way as his mind consisted of nothing other than what he felt.

He pressed against the thick warmth of his father's chest, and the people around him seemed to move closer. They spoke in high-pitched sounds that echoed the essence of the bright lights around them. His feelings of loneliness returned, and the slowly birthing gap between him and the world widened. The fissures began to cry out, searching from one side of the chasm to the other.

She had always been inside of him, and he had always been inside of her, but now, amongst the crowd of otherness, his mother was nowhere to be found. He wailed, pushing hard against his father's chest. Through his screams, through his newly discovered sorrow, she found him. Her hands pulled him close. His body moved inward. Her smell and her touch comforted him, weakening his sadness. Her love healed the gap that tore apart life. She kissed his skin, softening his thoughts into calm pools of serenity. She breathed gentle sounds into his ears. His loneliness vanished.

"Arthur," she whispered slowly.

Again and again.

"Arthur."

And with each echo of that peculiar sound.

"Arthur."

Was the end of his beginning.

"Arthur."

And the beginning of his end.

Her voice tore wide the valley of separation, yet it pacified the loneliness that arose within him. He was no longer the stream of life that poured through selfless senses but rather the one that perceived that endless flow.

Music played from far across the canyon of his thoughts. His mother gently swayed to the sounds of a tender melody. Arthur was alone but no longer lonely. Her love flew across the emptiness that now surrounded him, and it caressed his solitude into a deep and peaceful sleep.

Romance Of The Cosmos
Or, Good Morning And Good Night

There within the endless nothing were endless little somethings falling in love. The loneliness of space, the secrecy of not existing, had become too much. They wanted to be closer, wanted to touch one another, wanted to know that they were real. Desire drew them nearer as they felt themselves becoming more.

In fact, their love became so strong that their wants became their needs. Once the little somethings had decided to stop being alone, it seemed they could never be alone again. Their growing romance began to burn with passion. Closer and closer they all became until they lost themselves in each other. New forms of being were birthed from their union, and from their creation came love's consequence. It was pure energy, and it poured outward through the cosmos. Against this vibrant release, however, was the never-ending demand of desire pulling inward. And so the steady process was set in motion, the push and the pull of intercourse that would burn bright across the universe.

Time passed by in billions of years. Through the constant ages the light of love shined onward. Its radiance reached a sphere of blue that revolved around the romance. This sphere was Earth, and there the light met its offspring. Upon that lonely planet a strange new existence had formed. Ways of being had been born from the mixing of cause with its own effect. That which was love made love with itself.

It was an act known as life.

One form of life, of which there were many, had learned to turn the light of love into nourishment. This being's origin was a single seed buried within the ground. When it awoke from the soil, it lifted itself upwards to the blue sky above. Its small leaves fed from the light that shined upon them, while its roots absorbed nutrients from the rich earth below. Higher and higher the green plant grew, until its branches became thick and bore a bright red fruit.

Another form of life upon the earth had learned to use this plant for its own needs. These creatures were known to themselves as humans, and they had discovered that the bean inside these crimson fruits was quite useful. It gave their bodies energy and pleased their senses.

However, they believed that there were better ways of making life live than the way it had done for ages. Chemicals were made and sprayed upon the plants that bore the ripe red fruits. These substances made the plants grow abundant, but in strange ways changed the essence of how things lived. The humans then hired other humans to work within the fields where the plants were forced to grow. They toiled for very little and labored for very long. The beans would be pulled from the bright red fruits and packed in large containers, then shipped across the seas of Earth. The ships that carried them would go to distant countries, places humans imagined up to be separate from each other. There the beans were taken to factories where they would be roasted and ground and packed into cans by large machines that ran without life. The product of this endeavor would be sold by groups of humans to countless other humans around the world.

One particular can of beans, born from these many events, reached its final destination. From the light of love to the birth of life it had journeyed. Through the hands of humans and the movement of machines it had traveled. And now it sat upon the counter of a diner in the small Midwestern town of Moyenne, which was in the large imaginary outline called the United States of America.

A woman working as a waitress at the diner had prepared the beans in a way that many humans enjoyed. She dripped hot water through the grounds and into a large glass pitcher. She did this job nearly every day, all the while hating mostly everything because her life was stuck in tedious repeat.

As the dark liquid slowly dripped into the pot below, the waitress dreamt of how she really wanted her life to be. This was a common occurrence for most people in the world, and though it was an awful way to exist, it seemed to be the only choice.

The pot became full, and the waitress awoke to her current condition. She carried the drink to a table of three and poured the hot beverage into the cup of a dejected-looking young man. He drank the nearly black liquid, the product of countless connections that traveled across time and space.

"Tastes like shit," he said, setting the cup down.

"What'd you expect?" said the woman beside him.

14

"Coffee," he replied, "not shit."

The other, slightly older, man at the table reached past the woman and grabbed the cup of coffee. After taking a slow drink from it he returned it to the young man.

"It tastes all right," he said.

The twenty-something looked down into the dark reflection in his coffee. He wondered to himself what the point of everything was, which he knew was a clichéd and useless act. Nevertheless, he contemplated the question every day of his life, even if it was a futile thing to do. He felt that it was necessary in order to keep his integrity intact, as well as for the fact that the only inkling of an answer was that the meaning of it all was to look for the meaning of it all.

The young man's name was Oliver Radcliff, and he was by all accounts currently depressed. He wasn't always so, though he often did feel sad about his life. And it wasn't that he enjoyed being depressed, as seemed to be the case for many of the people he knew to be in such a state. It was simply that he felt he should be depressed, what with seeing no meaning in life and at the same time so much suffering in the world.

He knew that there shouldn't be sorrow when facing purposelessness, that it's the emptiness in existence that lets us paint our spirit upon it, but he just couldn't seem to get that understanding to coincide with his life. Instead he only saw how everything and everyone dies, which is a reasonably depressing thought if one hasn't embraced the fact of impermanence. And as for the suffering he saw in the world, which he felt both passionate and apathetic for at the same time, he considered himself completely powerless to eliminate it. He did what he could, though he didn't believe it to be much. In fact, he knew that he did very little at all. He was a vegetarian. He rarely drove his car. He recycled what plastics he bought. That was it.

To match his few virtues, he drowned himself in self-destructive egoism. He would often spend days sitting around in drunken contemplation, thinking about how his life could be better if he just had a different one. Night would come, and he would smoke away his thoughts into a place that burned of truth laced with neurosis.

Sitting beside Oliver were his two married friends, Mike and Michelle. When Oliver was a freshman in high school, he had entered his way into the friendship of an eccentric group of seniors. Mike was one of them, and he and Oliver quickly grew close. Mike enjoyed

Oliver's company because of his calm and peculiar disposition. Oliver enjoyed being around Mike because he talked about things most people his age didn't talk about, important things like death and reality and art. He also thought Mike was cool because he was Japanese. Oliver had grown tired of the ordinary sea of white people around him, a sea of which he was knowingly a part.

After graduation, Mike stayed in town to work as an electrician. It was at his job that he met Michelle. She had moved to Moyenne just that year and had gotten a job as the secretary at the Enright Electrical Company. It wasn't her dream job, but, as she told everyone, it paid the bills.

The two of them quickly fell in love and just as quickly decided to get married. At their wedding Mike confessed that it was Michelle's cold yet caring blue eyes that really pulled him in. It was also the tattoos that graced the most intimate parts of her body, though he didn't mention this at the occasion. Michelle said it was the way Mike walked that made her fall in love. Something about the way he bent his knees drove her crazy, which she admitted was a strange fondness. Both of them agreed that it was the entirety of the other that really made them fall in love, and so they joined their lives together into one.

"So what are you up to today?" Michelle asked, pulling Oliver slightly away from his thoughts.

"I'm gonna work on some stuff," he replied. "I haven't painted in a while."

"What're you gonna paint?"

"Stuff," he said, shrugging his shoulders.

The waitress returned with a large plate of pancakes. On top of them was a perfectly round dollop of bright, buttery-like substance that had begun to melt and slide about like an oily glacier.

"Pancakes," the waitress said to no one.

"Here," Mike answered, lifting his hand as if to awaken her to the fact that he existed.

"Can I get you anything else?" she asked listlessly as she set the plate down.

"No," Mike smiled. "Thank you very much."

She turned and left without a word.

"You should paint the Ganges," Michelle said to Oliver.

"I've never been," he replied.

"I know you've never been. Use our pictures."

"Eh."

"It was such a transcendent space."

"A painting from a photo might loose its transcendence."

"No, no, no," she replied, shaking her head. "You'd infuse it with your own sacredness, that unique style of yours. Plus it would look perfect in the hallway right outside Audrey's room."

"Maybe," he said before taking a drink of his coffee.

The three of them fell silent. Mike quickly ate his pancakes while Oliver and Michelle looked about the diner in a slight daze. The sun had begun to pour into the eastern windows, casting a warm, pink glow upon the objects it touched. It was early in the morning, though to them it was the end of the night. Mike and Michelle's three-year-old daughter, Audrey, was spending the weekend with her aunt, so the young parents' time of freedom had been utilized as profusely as possible. This had resulted in the three of them staying up until sunrise drinking cheap boxed wine, smoking two joints, listening to a pile of old records, and playing board games with new rules they made up on the spot. The final glorious moment of their night had occurred when Mike won a game of Mouse Trap by capturing not mice but cut out portraits of 19th century German philosophers pasted upon green plastic army men. Hegel was the only one to escape, thanks to a missing leg that brought about his fortunate tumble, though Mike swore he saw Schopenhauer give a shove from behind.

"I'm going home to sleep now," Oliver said suddenly, pulling out his wallet and setting a few bucks on the table. He reached across the shoulders of Michelle and Mike and pulled them in close. "I love you. Good night."

"Love you too, man," Mike replied, as Michelle made an affectionate purr to the both of them.

"Paint me Varanasi!" she begged as Oliver stood up.

"We'll see," he said, putting on his dark blue coat.

"Yes, we will," she replied with a smile.

He walked to the exit of the diner with a slow and heavy stride. An old woman at the counter smiled goodbye to him as he pressed his hands against the cold glass doors. With a push he felt the crisp air of an early winter morning against his skin.

The Universe At Play
Or, A Warm View Of The Cold

Faye held her brand new pen with pride and thought to herself how easy it was to have earned it. All she had needed to do was turn normal letters into swirly ones, which the teacher called writing in cursive. Her friends found this difficult. They couldn't seem to grasp that the letters hadn't really changed, other than just looking a little different. She had always thought letters were funny anyway. They weren't even real things. At least she had never seen one in person, which is what made things real to her.

She imagined meeting the letter B on the sidewalk outside of her house. He was big and fat and red with a funny-looking face on top. In his little, white-gloved hand he held a banana, because banana starts with B.

"Hello," she said kindly to him. "How are you?"

All he said back was, "Buh." That's all he would ever say back since that was the only sound Bs could make.

She pressed her pen down onto the open page of a notebook. As her hand moved the pen along, a seemingly magical trail of black ink was left behind.

Faye had earned this ability through her mastery of cursive, but she refused to let the maiden voyage of her ballpoint pen be destined for words. Instead, she poured out from her thoughts a picture. It was her father. He was standing tall atop a hill made of little jagged lines of grass. In his right hand he held the very pen that Faye had used to draw him. It even had the same giraffe-print pattern, though she admitted to herself that she had gotten some of the details off. Pouring out of the pen in his hand was an enchanted breeze of black ink that spun around the entire blue-lined page in thick, messy swirls.

She pulled out a small, pink bag from the compartment in her desk. From it she took a little, plastic stamp, which she pressed onto her drawing, leaving tiny red hearts cast amongst the swirls.

Her artwork was finished, and it was time for her pen to know the world of words. High atop the page, to the left of the tall red line, she wrote in large letters DAD. On the bottom right she crisscrossed a line into the shape of a star. Beside it she wrote her name.

Gently shutting her notebook and placing it back into her desk with her pink bag, she stood up and turned around to scan the classroom. It was break time, and she and her classmates had the freedom to do what they wanted.

She walked away from her desk and stood beside a short bookshelf that sat in the corner of the room. She stood just tall enough to see out the long windows above it, though the bottoms of them were covered in a layer of light snow. She felt cold staring outside, even though the room was kept quite warm.

"Faye can play!" her friend Jessica yelled from behind. She turned to see a group of girls sitting on the big, round carpet that was made to look like Earth.

"Take this," another girl said as Faye approached them. Suddenly in her hands was a paper cutout of a telephone. It was drawn in vivid blue ink. She felt jealous at the sight of its vibrant color, and then she felt sad for her black-inked pen sitting tucked away in her desk.

"Hello?" Jessica spoke into another paper telephone.

"Hello?" Faye replied, lifting the cutout to her face.

"Guess what?"

"What?"

"Chicken-butt!"

At this all the girls laughed, and Faye fell beside them on the Earth shaped rug. Scattered amongst them on the floor were more cutouts in blue ink, most of which were ordinary objects that the girls pretended to use.

A skillet with squiggles of eggs on top.

A hand mirror with the reflection of a smiling girl.

A toothbrush with a thick dollop of toothpaste.

Beside Faye sat a girl with cutouts of gloves taped to the palms of her hands. She waved them about with a smile on her face.

"Can I make one?" Faye asked the group.

"Here," one of them said, passing a piece of pale yellow construction paper her way, along with a pen that was pink with white dots. Though her pen may only have black ink, Faye thought it at least looked cooler than this one.

"Be careful with my pen!" yelled Lucy from across the circle.

"I will," Faye uttered as she stared at the blank page.

What could she make? It would have to impress the others. She wanted something funny, but also something only a smart person would make. Her pen fell down to the page just as an idea rose to her head. With slow and steady motions she drew a large rectangle, and within it a square and some dials to the right. On top of it she placed two squiggles with circles on their ends.

"Scissors?" she asked, holding out her hand. Someone passed her a pair and she got to work cutting out her drawing of a TV, the old-looking kind that she had never really seen before but knew to be what a drawing of a TV should look like. With much difficulty she succeeded in piercing the paper with the round-tipped scissors, cutting out the inside square so there was a hole where the screen would be.

Holding it up to her face, she tried to say something funny to the girls, but all she could do was laugh. They all stared at her and laughed too.

Mrs. Lawrence then yelled out to the class. Still holding the TV up to her face, Faye turned and stared across the room. She gazed through the paper at her teacher, as the other students ran up to their desks.

"My pen!" Lucy squealed, grabbing it from the ground and speed walking to her seat. Standing beside the chalkboard, Mrs. Lawrence turned her eyes to Faye and gave a smile.

"Let's go, Faye," she spoke across the room.

Returning to her desk, Faye placed the TV cutout in her notebook and pulled out her black-inked pen. She held it tight in her hand as she listened to her teacher talk about the world.

Our Life Amongst Others
Or, Who We Are

"I just don't get it," Megan laughed, shaking her head as she opened her locker.

"What's not to get?" Claire asked, standing beside her.

"Just because he eats meat?" Megan replied.

"It's gross."

"I eat meat. Am I gross?"

"A little, yeah."

"Well, screw you."

"Sorry."

"So you don't want to be with him because he eats cheeseburgers?"

"It's gross."

"Most people eat meat you know."

"Good for them."

Claire hated talking about her opinions. She knew everyone had their own ideas about the world and that most people thought that theirs were the truth. She'd rather just live by her own beliefs and let others do the same. She sometimes felt ashamed of this notion, though. How would the world change if nobody ever stood up for their beliefs? But then again maybe it would change, and for the better, if everyone kept to themselves.

"Well, I'm hungry," Megan said, shutting her locker, "and I'm going to go home and eat some meat."

"Enjoy that," Claire replied, thinking to herself about how much she didn't like her friend, yet at the same time how much she did.

"I will," Megan laughed back. "See you tomorrow, Claire."

"See you," Claire said, giving a half-smile and a half-wave. She turned away from Megan and started walking down the hallway full of students eagerly leaving school. A sea of voices in every pitch, tone, and intensity, the kind of sound found only among a mass of teenagers, flooded her ears and mixed with the echo of metal lockers slamming shut all around.

She felt cold thinking of the walk home ahead of her, which she looked forward to. Being cold was a pleasure for her. She liked feeling the frail warmth of her winter clothes wrapped around her body as the cold air froze the tip of her nose and flowed throughout her lungs. The sight of leafless trees and mounds of snow brought emotions up from deep within. To Claire, winter was a time of sincerity. It was when the world froze that she saw what was genuine about life. In the stillness she glimpsed what was real. She couldn't quite name what it was that she felt, but she knew that she felt it and that it was true.

She approached the wide doors of the school building. Holding a pile of books in her arms, she turned and pushed with her back against one of the glass doors. The air outside was dry and cold, and the sky was a bright, flat gray. Small groups of students with red faces stood around the parking lot, talking amongst themselves. As she walked past them, Claire noticed the small puffs of vapor that arose from the breath of their voices.

She thought about Drew and the way he had looked when she told him they couldn't be together. It wasn't that big of a deal really. They had only gone on one date. But she nonetheless felt kind of bad for ending it with him so quickly, and for such a peculiar reason. His face looked so sad and confused when she told him it was because he ate meat. She couldn't help it though. She kept picturing the way he looked on their date, his mouth full of cheeseburger, or, as she saw it, dead cow. She felt even worse when he offered to go vegetarian. She turned him down because she didn't want to be with someone who changed just for her.

Claire wondered how many vegetarian boys there were that were her age. Were there even any at all in Moyenne? Maybe she would just have to learn to kiss lips that also graced the flesh of dead animals.

All dating issues aside, she was glad her parents had raised her vegetarian. It was something to define herself by, and she knew that it was the right way to live. Even after her mother died, who, from what she was told, was the one who had convinced her father to stop eating meat, she and her siblings were still brought up as vegetarians. She remembered the countless times her father would cook them dinner and tell them that their health, along with the health of the world, was the most important thing to nourish.

As she approached the end of the parking lot she saw her brother walking down the sidewalk on the opposite side of the street. His long, thin limbs moved in a way that expressed just what Claire imagined him to be inside, which was alone.

"Oliver!" she yelled out as she hurried across the damp street.

He stopped and turned to face her. His face seemed neither happy nor sad, which rather comforted her. She enjoyed his apparent detachment. It gave her room to be herself, to express the opinions she purposely held away from others.

"Hello, Claire," he said with a light smile. "How are you?"

"I'm good," she answered, not having anything else to say.

"Good," he replied.

They walked together down the sidewalk half-covered in snow. His long legs made his pace much faster than hers, so she had to somewhat hurry to keep up with him.

"Where are you going?" she asked in between cold and heavy breaths.

"To the store," he replied.

"Oh."

"I need some things."

"It's cold out."

"Yeah."

"What are you getting?"

"Some food. I've got nothing at my place."

"Oh."

"I'll walk you home first."

"It's all right."

"No, I will. I've got nothing much else to do."

"Okay," she said as they stopped beside a busy street. They waited for the light to change in silence. She lost her attention as she stared down at her feet, and after some time of waiting she felt her brother's hand press against her back.

"It's changed," he said quietly.

They moved across the street and followed the sidewalks through town until they approached her house.

"Thanks," she said, turning to him. "Now go get yourself something to eat."

"I will," he replied. "Tell Dad and Faye I said hello, and Jeanne if she's there too."

"I will," she answered, turning to walk through the yard.

As she reached the porch she looked around to see her brother walking back down the way they came.

"Love you!" she yelled out to him.

"Love you," he said back just loud enough for her to hear.

She watched him walk in his sad-looking way until he could no longer be seen. She was alone, standing upon the porch of her house, and in the still solitude of winter she felt the sincere feeling that she couldn't define. It was a moment that she would for some reason always remember.

Embers In The Gray
Or, Lonely Thoughts When You're Not Alone

Oliver wondered what life was like to his father and sisters.

He imagined the worlds that they experienced. Were their minds flavored with the same peculiarities as his? Were their lives graced with similar perceptions and ideas? Was the bond of family a connection through which subjectivity was shared? Or were they simply humans with no relation aside from the blood in their veins?

And what about his dead mother?

What did she think about all of this?

He listened to the drone of distant cars behind the foreground of crunching snow beneath his feet. His thoughts caressed the idea that they were not alone, that they were not a solitary experience inside of his skull. He imagined a sea of consciousness flooding across eternity, formless minds weaving together a perception of the universe. Every life came from the same source, which Oliver imagined to be nothingness. These sibling lives would always be separate in their little molecules of mind. The emptiness from which they came would be the barrier between their skins. Only through their ebbing and flowing could their seclusion become the unity of their past. Through the push and pull of life they created the universe, the universe from which they were originally born.

Oliver lost himself in thought. His ideas, which spoke within his mind the poetry of truth, mesmerized him away from reality. Instead of seeing, feeling, experiencing what he believed to be true, he merely thought about it inside his lonely head. If he would only open his eyes could he see the beauty of the world he dreamt of.

The distant sound of cars became not so distant, awakening Oliver back into his world. In front of him was the dark, wet pavement of John Luke Street.

After collecting his thoughts and waiting for the light to change, he moved his way across the intersection of bright headlights. Moger's Supermarket sat heavily in front of him, its well-lit sign shining red through the delicate snow beginning to fall. The sun had already begun to set, and the world was fading into a dark shade of gray. As Oliver walked his way up the busy parking lot his eyes darted around at the various people coming and going from the store. He felt a sensation inside of him that he knew well, a sensation that he had learned to hate. It was a deeply buried cynicism mixed with contempt for all the people around him. He knew that it would quickly grow into proportions that included not just those nearby but all of humanity. It was a feeling that often arose when he found himself surrounded by consumerism. He hated the feeling because he didn't want to despise people, but he was nevertheless accepting of the angry truth that it yelled into his head. The economic way of life that people had created was destroying the world, and he in turn loathed not just the inane act of buying and selling things, which for the most part were just pointless diversions from life, but also the people involved in the act. The thought never occurred to him that maybe this disgust arose because he was projecting his self-contempt upon those around him. After all, he was there shopping too.

The glass doors of the grocery store slid out of Oliver's way as he walked into the building. Once inside, he rummaged through his head for the few things he needed. With a wide-eyed yet detached gaze he quickly walked up and down aisles. He collected what he came there for while keeping entirely to himself. This wasn't much different from those around him, since most people prefer to avoid any unnecessary interactions with strangers. The modern human often goes bumping around the universe while never leaving the confines of the little world inside their skull.

Oliver stopped himself in the snack aisle to stare at the rows of large vibrant bags of what could hardly be called food. He felt his contempt surge, yet he forced the feeling aside. What could be said about the American diet that hasn't been said before? What anger within him could change the eating habits of a nation? He laughed a quiet laugh to himself that was directed not only at the world but also at his own self-righteous being.

He finished getting what he needed and checked out at the self-service register, which was available to customers so as to provide them with the least amount of social interaction possible. He paid with a credit card, which he hated but nonetheless used. It was one of the many things he disliked about the way he lived and one of the many things he did nothing at all to change.

Far above Moger's Supermarket, while Oliver scanned his life away in boredom one item at a time, molecules of water were feeling rather cold. Their bodies became rigid as they drifted about the air, colliding with one another and attaching in unique ways. These evolving communities of ice began to grow heavy—so heavy, in fact, that they no longer seemed to be lighter than the air. To this they gave in and began their beautiful decent, one with an elegance that exposed the frozen water's remnants of eternal grace.

As the snow danced its way to the ground, feeling the pull of love it had forever known, Oliver left the sliding glass doors of the supermarket, feeling yet again depressed. He found no joy that wasn't swallowed whole by the problems of the world, problems that he felt unable to fix. He questioned if he was really that passionate for the well-being of others. Was he merely sad about his own life, his own apathy, and his own despair? Was the corruption of the world around him upsetting only because it was happening to the world in which he must live?

Holding his bag of groceries in one hand, he pulled a pack of cigarettes out of his coat pocket with the other. He stared at his surroundings as he took out a cigarette and placed it between his lips. He walked a little ways alongside the store, stopping in a spot where the lights didn't shine. Lighting his cigarette with a yellow plastic lighter, he watched to his right as people moved busily across the parking lot. As he blew out a cloud of smoke he tried to push away his anger. He turned to his left to stare at the darkness beside him. A small, dark alley led down the side of the building, and on the other side of it sat a thick cluster of trees. The black shapes of their limbs hung in the snowy sky as the artificial glow of lights singed at their edges.

Oliver took a heavy drag from his cigarette and imagined what he looked like from afar. He saw himself standing there amongst the cold gray scene. The smoke was leaving his lips in a way that spoke his disheartened emotions. The warm halo of his cigarette made him stand out from the ashen surroundings. He hoped that in reality he looked as he did in his head. This notion made him feel satisfied, which made him feel conceited, which made him feel sad again, which made him take another drag from his cigarette.

The snow fell heavy as Oliver walked out of the picture in his head. The image, however, remained without him there like a perfect moment in time.

December 24th, 1965
Or, After And Before

Arthur sat alone, bathed in the color-changing light that radiated from behind the nearby aluminum Christmas tree. In his hands he played with a small plastic airplane, which his uncle Walt had given him just a few hours ago. It was gray and white with two red stars on the tops of its wings. Arthur could tell it was hollow when he shook it in his hand and knocked it against his knee. He wondered what it was like inside.

Raising the toy plane high above his head, he watched it change colors with the light of the room. Arthur imagined himself inside of it, pushing the buttons and pulling the levers that lined its cockpit. He sat in the pilot's seat and gazed out of the plane's wide windows as the horizon changed from green to blue to gold to red and back again to blue.

His mother and father were talking in the other room. As their voices got louder Arthur was pulled from the inside of his plane and back onto the living room floor. He couldn't quite understand what his parents were talking about, or rather he didn't seem to have the ability to listen. His thoughts were replaying the earlier moment when his uncle Walt gave him the present.

"I used to fly one of these," his uncle had said, handing him the toy plane wrapped in a thin red bow. "Maybe someday you will too."

Arthur imagined he was back in the cockpit, except this time his uncle sat beside him. They both wore uniforms like the kind Arthur had seen on his cousin's new G.I. Joe.

"This is no good," Walt complained, staring into a small screen that beeped every few seconds. "No good at all. They're coming up on us."

Arthur yanked at the controls in front of him and the plane spun around in the blue sky. He could see the enemy in the distance as the sun began to set into a deep gold.

"We can handle these guys," his uncle said, turning to him with a sharp smile. "Can't we, boy?"

And as the enemy planes moved closer the sky burned red.

"No," his uncle grumbled. "No, no, no. Not that!"

They were blinded by green light as a loud voice rang out.

"Arthur!" his father yelled. "You need to get ready for bed, son. You-know-who's coming tonight, and unless you get to sleep he might just pass right on by."

Arthur turned to see his father standing in the doorway as he changed from green to blue. His mother came up beside him and wrapped her arms around his waist.

"What do you want Santa to bring you, Arthur?" she asked. He thought about what he wanted, but couldn't name one thing. What would he get if he didn't know what he wanted? Would he even get anything at all?

"I dunno," he mumbled while looking down at the plane in his hands.

"You don't know!" his father laughed. "We'll I'm sure Santa knows, and I'm sure you'll like what you get."

"Let's go get you ready for bed," his mother said, letting go of his father. Arthur quickly stood to his feet and darted for his bedroom. As he stepped into his room he reached high upon the wall and switched on the lights. This was a new feat he had just recently achieved, and it made him happy every time he saw the flood of light that he created.

He walked to the dresser that sat in the corner of his room, and pulling open the bottom drawer, he took out his white pajamas. He pulled off the fancy clothes he had worn for his family's Christmas party and threw them on the ground at his feet.

"You pick those up and fold them," his mother said from behind, surprising him.

"Yes ma'am," he replied, dropping his pajamas to the ground and bending over to fold his clothes, all the while bare-naked.

"Good," she said as he finished. He grabbed his pajamas and sat with a thud on the ground. Holding the pants at his feet, he kicked his legs upwards through the soft cotton. He grabbed his shirt and, standing up, pulled it over his head. After finding his arms through the sleeves he felt that something wasn't quite right.

"It's backwards, Arthur," his mother said from the doorway.

"Oh," he groaned, pulling his arms back in through the sleeves. He twisted his body and the shirt about until it seemed that everything was facing the right way.

"There you go," his mother laughed, turning away from the doorway. "Come on."

He walked with her down the narrow hallway that led to the bathroom. His hand ran along the smooth, green wallpaper, sliding up and down like waves. He could smell the scent he loved more than any other as he moved closer to his mother. It made him feel less alone, though he didn't really realize it. He wasn't even sure what being lonely felt like, though it was an emotion he felt quite often.

The bathroom lights buzzed to life as his mother flicked the switch upon the wall. Arthur pulled the small, metal stool from the corner of the room, skidding it along the tile floor until it rested in front of the sink. He stepped upon it and turned to his mother.

"Here," she said, handing him his toothbrush. A blob of light green paste sat atop its bristles. Arthur held the brush in front of his eyes and stared with disgust at the toothpaste. He hated the taste of it, yet he knew that it was inescapable.

"Brush," his mother commanded.

And so he did.

"Spit," she said after what to him felt like quite some time. He tilted his body forward and let loose the foamy green that had accumulated in his mouth. He watched as it gathered around the drain and slowly swirled about. His mother turned on the water, which washed away the frothy mixture of toothpaste and spit. Arthur held his hands like a bowl beneath the faucet and stared as a lake arose in his palms. He moved his hands away from the stream and tried with all his might to keep the water within his grasp, but as he had discovered many times before, no matter how hard he pressed his fingers together the water would slip away. He gave up and collected another bowl of water to rinse out his mouth. After spitting the water away he jumped down from his stool and slid it back into the corner.

"Does Santa brush his teeth?" he asked his mother.

"Of course he does," she answered, bending over and picking him up. "Everyone brushes their teeth."

"What about the Tooth Fairy?"

"Well, she has to."

"Why?"

"Because teeth are her specialty. She has to set a good example for all the kids around the world."

"Wouldn't she want people to lose their teeth?"

"Why would she want that?"

"So she could have more of them."

"Good people don't use other people for their own benefit, Arthur. Besides, she would never get any more nickels if everyone lost their teeth."

"Oh, yeah."

"Good people want to help others, not themselves."

"I want to be a good person."

"You are," his mother said, laying him down in his bed. He was almost unaware of moving from the bathroom back into his bedroom. She pulled the blankets across his body and rubbed her hand through his hair.

"Is Dad a good person?" he asked.

"Yes, he is," she told him. "I think he's a very good man."

"Does he help others?"

"He helps you and me, doesn't he?"

"Yeah," he answered while rubbing his feet up and down the sheets of his bed. His thoughts returned to Santa Claus and the fact that he would be coming tonight.

"Since I'm a good person," he asked, looking into his mother's brown eyes, "will Santa bring me what I want?"

"Well, you don't know what you want, Arthur," she replied, shaking her head.

"I do know what I want."

"And what is that?"

"A pup!"

"You want a dog? I'm not sure Santa could give you one of those."

"Why?" he asked upset.

"You're not old enough," his mother answered, "and you didn't give him enough time. You have to let Santa know what you want before Christmas Eve. Think of all the kids he has to give presents to. He's probably already planning for next Christmas."

"So does that mean if I'm good I'll get a pup next Christmas?" he asked her excitedly.

"We'll see," she said with a smile.

"I think I hear sleigh bells!" his father's voice rang out from across the house, which made Arthur's eyes open wide.

"You'd better get to sleep," his mother told him before kissing his forehead.

He nodded yes and pulled his blankets up high, watching as his mother walked away. She stopped within the doorway of his room and turned around.

"Good night, Arthur," she whispered.

"Good night," he said back.

"I love you."

"I love you too."

She flipped off the lights and slipped away, pulling his bedroom door nearly shut. A small sliver of light entered the room through the crack she left open. Arthur stared up at the darkness of the ceiling. He imagined Santa above him, walking along on the snow-covered roof. He saw his sleigh and his reindeer as they sat waiting for Santa to return.

The image at first brought excitement, but then it turned into a subtle fear. Arthur felt the realness of a man that had the power to fly across the world and see inside the thoughts of children. Sure, by his mother's definition Santa was a good person. He did good things for other people and never did anything bad. But it still made Arthur feel afraid knowing that there was someone out there with that much power. What if Santa changed his mind? What if he didn't want to help people anymore?

Arthur slowly fell asleep to thoughts that tried to keep him awake. His parents sat together in the living room, bathed in the color-changing light that shone from behind the Christmas tree.

"He wants a dog," she said.

"Let's get him one next year," he replied.

"He'll be six," she whispered. "Six years old…"

"And you'll be twenty-six," he quietly laughed back.

"Let's not talk about my age," she whispered in his ear, climbing on top of him as the room slowly turned from red to green to blue to gold and then back to red all over again.

Someday You Will Die
Or, Being Alive

"It doesn't matter what happens to them."

"What does matter then?"

"That we get out of here alive, together"

"You're forgetting that I'm already dead."

"You know what I mean. Let's go."

"No. I'm done running. We can end this now. All of it."

"What's going on?" Faye asked her sister.

"What?" Claire replied.

"What are they doing?" Faye asked, crawling along the ground towards the television.

"It's a show," Claire answered. "They're vampires."

"Oh," Faye replied, rolling about the floor.

"I want you to live with me forever."

"But you won't change me."

"I will."

"Then do it now."

"What's a vampire?" Faye asked, spinning around to face her sister. Claire sat crossed-legged on the couch, staring at the television and ignoring the question.

"Hey, what's a vampire?" Faye asked again.

"Someone who never d—"

"Turn that stuff off, Claire," her father sounded out from the next room, cutting off her words.

"Faye," Claire said to her sister, "go to the kitchen."

"Why?"

"Because I want to watch this, and you can't."

"Oh, okay. Why can't I watch it?"

"You're not old enough."

"And you are?"

"Yes. Now go, please. Maybe Dad needs help in the kitchen."

"I do," he said from the doorway. "You wanna help me finish dinner, Faye?"

"I'm coming!" she yelled out. She stood and ran to her father's side, following him into the brightly lit kitchen, where it smelled of onions and other foods Faye couldn't quite distinguish.

"It stinks in here," she said.

"Well, thank you," her father replied with a smile.

"What're you making, Dad?" she asked.

"Tacos!" he shouted, stirring something on the stove.

"Tacos are okay," she said, sitting upon a kitchen chair.

"Okay works for me as long as you eat it," he said, turning to her. "Can you get the lettuce ready for me?" She happily nodded yes. "Good!" he replied. "But go clean your hands first."

She jumped from her chair and ran to the bathroom down the hall, where after some effort she managed to reach the sink and wash her hands. As she returned to the kitchen she saw that her father had placed a head of lettuce upon the kitchen table.

"Can you rip it up into little pieces for me?" he asked.

She nodded yes as she returned to her chair, where the round ball of green sat in front of her upon the table. She pulled off its slippery outer leaf and held it in her hand. The light glistened through its thin skin, and she stared at its veins of pale green.

"What is lettuce?" she asked her father.

"It's a plant," he answered. "A vegetable."

"What's a plant?" she asked.

"You know what a plant is."

"But tell me anyway."

"Well," he said, pausing to think, "it's a living thing, like you and me. But it doesn't think or feel. It grows from the Earth and just lives right where it popped out of the ground. Most of them get used by us animals. In fact, I'd say plants want to be eaten."

"Why would a plant want that?" she asked, pulling a small corner off of the leaf and placing it on the plate beside her.

"So it can help others live," he replied. "So we can eat it, and it can become a part of us, and together we can grow."

"Oh," she said, pulling another small bit off of the lettuce, "Then we don't eat animals because they don't want to help others live?"

"Well, we don't eat animals because they can think and feel," he answered, returning to cooking what was upon the stove. "And it's just kinda mean, don't you think?"

"Yeah," she answered, continuing her job of shredding the lettuce.

After a long moment of silence, Faye had built up a small pile of green bits upon her plate. As she continued to pile more of them up, she wondered whether or not plants really couldn't think or feel. Just because they couldn't show people that they did, she thought, doesn't mean that they don't. But if she couldn't eat vegetables either, what could she eat?

"Dad!" Claire yelled out from the front room. "Come here!"

He quickly wiped his hands on a kitchen towel and walked into the living room. On the TV was a broadcast with the words BREAKING NEWS in bright red letters across the top. The reporter was wearing a raincoat and standing in front of a backdrop of what looked like emergency crews moving quickly through a downpour of rain.

"*No official word yet on exactly how may people this may have affected,*" the man said with a serious yet theatrically compassionate tone, "*but from estimates we can say that there could be an upwards of twenty dead and dozens injured.*"

"*What kind of atmosphere do you feel there, Steve?*" an excessively enunciated woman's voice asked.

"*It's one of severe solemnity,*" Steve answered with a dramatic pause, "*and unbreakable courage to face what has happened here today.*"

Suddenly a bright yellow banner of words appeared across the bottom of the screen. It read in bold, black letters TWO BOMBS DETONATE IN SUBWAY STATION.

"It's pretty bad," Claire said. Her father walked closer to the television and stared in grief at the news report. Behind him crept Faye. She watched from around the corner of the sofa as the news reporter spoke too quickly for her to understand. Only a few scattered words made it into her head, words like bomb, subway, people, and dead.

Dead was a word that she has heard before and only slightly understood. From what she knew most things died. Vegetables died. Animals died. People died. She wasn't really sure what dying meant though.

"What does dead mean?" she asked her father and sister.

"It means to stop living," Claire answered, turning to Faye, who sat upon the floor.

"It means," her father added, moving close to Faye, "that someone has to leave this life behind."

"And go somewhere else?" Faye asked.

"Maybe," he answered.

"Or maybe not," Claire said.

"What?" Faye asked.

"What she means is we don't really know what happens after someone dies," her father said, sitting down on the sofa and lifting Faye up to his lap.

"*While officials still remain quiet on the suspect,*" the news anchor spoke facing the camera, "*serious concern is in the air over the prospect of foreign terrorist organizations being behind such a dreadful and catastrophic event.*"

"What happened?" Faye asked, looking up into her father's eyes. He shook his head and patted his hand upon her lap.

"Someone did something bad," he said, "and people got hurt."

"Did they die?" she quietly asked.

"Some did, yes."

"Why?"

"Because when people get hurt too much, they die."

"So people should try to not get hurt."

"That's right."

"So then they would never die?"

"Well," he paused, "everyone dies. We all grow old and someday pass away. But most people don't die for a long, long time."

"Everyone dies?" she asked, stressing her words.

Her father slowly nodded yes.

"Will you die?" she asked him.

"Someday."

"And Claire?"

"Yes."

"And me?"

"Not for a very long time from now."

"Oh," she uttered, staring blankly at the television. Her thoughts tried to grasp this difficult new concept. Her young mind attempted to realize its own mortality. It didn't seem possible. She had always existed. How could she ever stop existing?

"This is awful," Claire said, continuing to watch the news report. Some people sitting around a desk were speculating as to the cause of the incident.

"We have to finish those tacos, Faye," her father said. He lifted her up and walked towards the kitchen. He stopped in the doorway and turned around. "Don't watch too much of this, Claire. It is awful, and you should keep the people who got hurt in your thoughts, but don't watch too much of the news. They turn this stuff into entertainment."

"Okay, Dad," she replied, half-listening to what he said.

Faye's thoughts were still trying to wrap themselves around what it meant to die, though the idea of it soon left her head. It was as if her unconscious knew that it was too much for her to handle, letting the task of helping her father take over her mind. However, something remained. Inside of her, with its roots buried deep, was a seed that would soon blossom into a flower of life and death.

Background
Or, Somewhat There

Oliver liked his job.

He also hated it.

It was never too difficult. He pretty much just had to show up on time and be there until he was able to leave. Sometimes a situation would occur that almost reached the point of becoming slightly challenging, like the time he had to explain to an angry mother why her son wasn't allowed in the store anymore.

The boy had been caught touching himself while gazing at the cover of a softcore movie entitled *Her Lust For Money*. The mother refused to believe Oliver and picked a fight with him over her son's innocence. The altercation was easily resolved by Oliver's ability to detach himself from whatever was going on around him. He became an indifferent sponge for her anger. In fact, within his head he enjoyed the situation. He had actually seen the movie long before when he was twelve years old. He had spent the night at a friend's house, and they had stayed up late watching action movies on TV. Long after his friend had fallen asleep, Oliver changed the channel and watched, with the volume turned all the way down, a movie about a woman from Texas who seduced different men for their money. He assumed she was from Texas because she always seemed to wear a cowboy hat, even when she was fucking in just the right way as to keep the camera from seeing what Oliver wanted to see so badly.

He had touched himself too, but at least it was in the privacy of his friend's living room at three in the morning.

Oliver's job was also somewhat enjoyable, albeit often boring. Most of his time was spent organizing shelves, which meant gazing at the covers of old books, albums, and movies while he placed them somewhere neatly in the store.

His hunger for collecting old books, albums, and movies often led him to buy a lot of what he stared at. His apartment was half full of things he had brought home from work. Each one of them was an escape from life, yet many also led him deeper into it.

His walls were covered in books that he had read, would like to read, or never really planned on reading at all. He had boxes full of albums in the same manner, though he was even more unlikely to actually use them. Tall racks of movies sat beside his old TV set, and a few were always scattered on the floor nearby.

Oliver hated his job for two reasons.

The first being that he liked it.

He didn't want to like it.

He wanted to hate it.

He wanted to do something else with his life, something eccentric, bizarre, adventurous. But his contentment with what he was doing often flattened out his dreams. He woke up every morning mostly able to face the day ahead, which was agreeable enough for his apathetic attitude to drift stagnantly by.

The second reason he hated the job was that it wasn't what he told himself and everyone else what he was supposed to do with his life. He was meant to be a painter. He was supposed to be in galleries and exhibitions around the world, not stacking books on shelves in a dusty old store in Moyenne.

When Oliver graduated high school he made the decision to follow his dreams of being an artist. The logical decision at the time was to go to art school. Within the first year of being there he dropped out. He told everyone that what he wanted to do couldn't be taught in classes. He would instead make it on his own.

He painted nearly every day for the first few years afterwards, but slowly comfort crept up on him. Days would come and go without him even touching a paintbrush. Eventually he would often deride the idea of being a painter. He told himself he could be happy here and now if he would just forget his goals and simply drift through life. In feverish bursts, however, his passion would return, often accompanied by some sort of intoxication, be it through drugs or simply experiencing life.

"I'll see you Monday," Sasha told Oliver as he was closing up the store. He stared at her ass as she walked away, criticizing himself the entire time for doing so.

He locked the door and walked to his car. It was dark out, yet the parking lot was brightly lit by the numerous lights that scattered the pavement. Sasha pulled away from the parking spot across from his. He remembered the way her ass looked as she walked away, and he again ridiculed himself for being too human.

"Dammit," he spoke aloud, directing the words at himself and at the conundrum of desiring what his mind wished he didn't. It's not that he believed sex was a bad. It was that he wanted sacredness within his life. He wanted to change his existence from that of a horny twenty-something white guy into that of a genuinely alive human being, moving with integrity and control through reality.

It was hard to do with thoughts of Sasha's ass in his head.

He pulled out his cell phone and texted Eric. His phone was out of date so he had to spell the words by punching numbers over and over again. He was the last person he knew of in his circle of friends that didn't have a smartphone. He refused to get one because he believed they took away from life more than they gave. He also held on strongly to the self-righteous honor he felt he deserved for not owning a better phone. It made him feel superior to be technologically inferior.

He started his car and pulled away. Driving down streets covered in old, wet snow, he neglected to realize that his radio was slightly on. He didn't notice that a song was in the air, but his unconscious mind listened to the entirety of "The End" by the Doors. It made him feel confusedly sad about existing, and by the time he reached Eric's house he was somewhat depressed about life.

"How's it goin'?" he asked as his friend sat down in the passenger seat.

"It's goin'," Eric replied. "You?"

"Yup," Oliver answered, pulling away.

The two of them unknowingly listened to various classic rock songs on their way to Oliver's apartment. This put them into a sort of reckless mood that made them want to forget their nine-to-fives and party through the whole weekend.

Oliver lit up a cigarette as he pulled into a parking spot outside his apartment. Like rock stars, he and Eric got out of his 1990 Buick Estate. They climbed the steps to Oliver's apartment and stood in the December night air. Oliver pulled out his keys and looked for the one to his door.

"You have anything to drink?" Eric asked, waiting on Oliver.

"Yeah," Oliver said between drags from his cigarette. He clumsily worked at the lock. "But I'm not drinking tonight."

"Oh yeah? Why?" Eric asked, putting his hands in his pockets and moving about restlessly. "And open the damn door. It's freezing out here."

"I'm trying. And I don't feel like feeling like shit."

"Whatever. I suppose you'll smoke then?"

"You supposed correctly. You should join me."

"No way. I don't feel like feeling like shit."

"Just because you freaked out last time," Oliver said as he finally got his door to unlock, "doesn't mean you will every time."

"Yeah, well, I have to think about my job, anyway," Eric said, quickly moving in through the door, "They don't exactly look highly upon that sort of thing. Enough of the students are doing it as it is. They don't need the faculty getting blazed too."

"Well, I can guarantee one member of your faculty gets high," Oliver said, taking off his jacket.

"Your dad does not get stoned."

"Maybe not, but I know he used to. Who majors in creative writing with a minor in philosophy, writes a book about lucid dreaming, and names his children Oliver, Faye, and Claire without ever getting stoned?"

"Who hasn't gotten high before? So maybe he tried it once or twice. From what I know of him he was no stoner."

"From what I know of him, which is our entire life together as father and son, he was a stoner."

"Whatever," Eric said, opening a cabinet in the kitchen and pulling out a half-empty fifth of vodka. "You care if I drink this?"

"Go ahead," Oliver replied, walking into another room. "There's some tonic in the fridge. Or orange juice if you want."

Eric poured himself a drink and sat down on the black sofa in Oliver's living room. He held the glass in front of his eyes and watched as the glow of lights mixed with the dark gray color of the walls, bouncing through the ice in his vodka tonic. He quickly drank while Oliver, in the other room, made the familiar noise of pulling out his stash and packing a bowl.

"Still hiding it in the same place?" Eric shouted, referring to the worn out old case that Oliver always kept his weed in. It was the box for *Little Nemo: The Dream Master* on the NES. He had found it at work one day in a moment that brought forth forgotten memories of playing the game when he was a child. He had decided on the spot that it would be a perfect match for the job. He treated it with great respect, never furthering the damage it had seen in years gone by.

"Yup," is all Oliver replied.

Eric shook his drink around and shot back what was left of it. He moved to the kitchen and made another. Oliver returned just as he finished.

"Let's go to the other room," he told Eric, motioning his head down the hallway. They walked into the small room in the corner of Oliver's apartment. Inside they sat on the scattered floor pillows that were lying around. Oliver turned on the stereo beside them and gazed at the boxes of records he had sitting along the wall. He slid out a white, unmarked album and placed the record upon the turntable. A click, thud, and hiss led the way into the sound of a soft, yet stirring, drumbeat. It was floating amongst the strums of a warm acoustic melody.

A flick of his thumb and Oliver set loose the quick sparks of his lighter. These small flames of metal hurled themselves haphazardly outward as a stream of butane escaped its plastic home. As chemicals collided in eccentric affairs, the molecular world was torn apart into a state of organized chaos. Fire came forth from this reaction and struck against the soft green body of *Cannabis sativa*, a plant that grew from the love that burned across the universe. The dried plant burst into flames, sending out various beautiful chemicals. These drifted through the hot air until the lungs of Oliver pulled them away.

As these unique formations of molecules entered Oliver's lungs, they were swept along his bloodlines and into his brain. It was there that they found their home.

Tetrahydrocannabinol, the most revered of these compounds, nestled itself in the parts of Oliver that were made just for this moment. Within his brain they made him change in extraordinary ways. His mind began to open up to the world that was around him, and at the same time it began to delve deeper into his internal existence. Just as these biological events were beginning to unfold, a peculiar thought came into his head.

"Just what is music?" he asked Eric, who was partaking in a much different chemical reaction.

"Oh boy," he replied. "I need another drink."

"No really, what is it?"

"It's sound organized into rhythms and melodies."

"No, it's more than that."

"What is it then?"

"It's the auditory expression of time. Think about it. If there wasn't time, there couldn't be music. You can't have a song that consist of one single instant."

"Wouldn't you say that's a subjective opinion?"

"Oh. Well, maybe."

"I'm getting another drink."

Oliver sat confused on the floor as Eric stood up and left the room. He was sure that he was on to something, though it seemed he had forgotten just what it was. He began to feel a little anxious just because he existed. He felt himself being too much of a living being, one that could die at any moment. He had to calm down by losing himself to the music. The organized sound of rhythm and melody had changed into a steady progression that seemed to move the moment forward. The drums pushed Oliver's body into a place that felt alive, and the ambient chords lifted his mind into a mesmerized state.

Eric laughed as he returned to the room.

"What?" Oliver asked.

"You're dancing," he replied, "and I spilled vodka on your kitchen floor."

"Thanks."

"If I have to listen to any more of the awful fucking music that's going around these days I'm going to kill myself," Eric complained as he clumsily sat down on the floor.

"This?" Oliver asked.

"No, no. This is okay. It's that damn robotic, repetitive, idiotic, pop crap that gets spewed onto the radio. I hear it all day. Do people actually like it?"

"I guess so. Why else would it be so popular?"

"And the lyrics. They're awful."

"The last song I heard had some computerized voice screaming a single note over and over," Oliver said as his dancing began to slow down to a stop. "And some plastic girl was singing about getting drunk and fucking everyone."

"That's pretty much it," Eric said, afterwards taking a long drink from his newly filled glass.

"I don't think people actually like it," Oliver said while staring at all the details of the room. His eyes followed the line of white Christmas lights that had always hung around the ceiling. He turned to face Eric and became enthralled by the clear ice in his glass. After a moment he pulled himself away from the trance and back to his train of thought. "I think people are made to believe they like it. It's just what they're supposed to do. Throw some noise onto a steady beat, put some famous person in front of it, and you have a so-called song to feed to everyone. And devour we do. Even if it makes us sick we'll eat away at the noise."

"Deep," is all Eric said back.

"It's that way with most things we do," Oliver continued. "We just take what we're given, even if deep down we don't really like it. Eventually it changes us and we grow to a point were we have to have it. Like all this Internet and cell phone shit."

"I like my cell phone," Eric replied, "and my Internet."

"Don't get me wrong. The Internet can be used for wonderful things. But is it? No. At least not for the most part. A majority of it's used to show everyone else how awesome our ordinary lives are, how funny some stupid bullshit is, or, of course, as a means to erect our penises."

"Why do you think I like it so much?" Eric laughed.

"Oh fuck you," Oliver joked.

The two sat in silence for a while, listening to the music until the record reached its end.

"We gotta do something," Eric said, standing up. "I'm restless." In his mind he was oblivious to the flashback of classic rock songs that had quietly entered his senses on the way over. He felt the need to be young, to party all weekend, and to show a woman how much of a man he was.

"Whatcha wanna do?" Oliver asked, though he was reluctant to really do anything.

"Let's go to Chuck's."

"No way. I'm not going to that damn bar."

"I can call Drew. He can give us a ride."

"I don't want to be at a bar right now, man."

"Well, too bad. You shouldn't have gotten high as hell."

"Come on. Just call Drew and have him come over. We can play some games or something."

"Dammit."

"Come on," Oliver lazily begged.

"Okay, whatever," Eric conceded. "But I'm drinking more of your liquor."

"Go ahead," he replied, standing up and heading out to his balcony. "I'm having a cigarette."

Oliver stood outside in the cold, smoking a cigarette and thinking about the darkness around and within him. He didn't really want to smoke a cigarette. He just felt he needed to in order to be brooding. He suffered the need to do a lot of things he didn't really want to do.

Within a few hours he would be drunk and stoned, throwing up at a bar he hated and wishing that he could learn to control the voice inside his head. It told him to go ahead and do it. Go ahead and find some truth within a lie. Oliver hoped that somewhere in the pain of intoxication he would see the light, but he always ended up in a place a little darker than before.

Me
Or, You

Claire watched her father's girlfriend, Jeanne, bustle around the living room, placing little red and green trinkets upon any open surface she could find. Claire noticed the way her hips moved funny when she stepped with her left leg. It wasn't very pronounced, just a little jut to her side. Claire wondered what caused this. Was it in an accident when she was younger? Or was it just a side effect of growing old? When Jeanne reached up to hang a wreath Claire stared at the skin of her waist as it slid out beneath the bottom of her shirt. It seemed softer than the rest of her body, though it did sag just a little. When Jeanne bent down into a box of decorations Claire looked through the gap in her collar as her shirt hung low. She saw Jeanne's breasts pressing against her black silk bra. The skin of her chest seemed more aged than that of her hips, and the sight of it moved Claire in a peculiar way. She felt connected with someone who was simply another human being. It was a glimpse into a future form of Claire's life as a living, aging body.

"Did you make this?" Jeanne asked, holding up a white cloth star with candy canes painted on it. "Yup, there's your name on the back," she said before Claire could answer. She set it down on the table beside her and continued to rummage through the box.

"I made it in second grade," Claire said, standing up. "Oliver did too." She kneeled down beside Jeanne and dug her hands into the box, pulling out a blue felt star with black and gold puff balls poorly glued to the front. She stood and smiled. "Not very Christmassy, but it's got a certain charm."

"We should make some decorations," Jeanne said excitedly, though Claire thought it seemed a bit insincere.

"We should," Claire replied with a smile. Jeanne was kind, and she treated Claire's father with love. She made him happy, and for that she was accepted into the family.

As the two of them continued to look through the box of holiday decorations, Faye walked through the room with a silent, yet heavy, presence.

"What's wrong?" Jeanne asked, knowing that something was bothering the seven-year-old girl.

"Nothing," Faye replied.

"Okay then," said Jeanne. "Do you want to help us?"

"No, I'm busy."

"What're you up to?"

"I'm thinking," Faye mumbled, leaving the room.

"What does a seven-year-old have to think about so deeply?" Jeanne asked, sitting down on the living room sofa.

"Lots of stuff," Claire answered. "I remember becoming obsessed with the strangest things when I was young. Once I was stuck on the idea that above me was endless outer space. All around Earth was a whole lot of nothing. I imagine what went on in my head didn't make much sense, but I do remember spending hours just thinking about it. I mean, imagine all the things a child could dream up existing out there."

"So what's Faye caught up on then?"

"Could be anything. But she did see the news last night."

"Really? The bombing?" Jeanne tilted her head and made a sad expression, pressing the palms of her hands on her legs to seemingly steady herself. "That's probably it."

"She asked us what death was," Claire told her, after which Jeanne looked stunned. "She seemed to forget about it though."

"Poor thing," Jeanne quietly said.

"I'll keep an eye on her. Don't worry."

"Your father needs to talk to her about it."

"I'm sure he will. Speaking of, have you gotten anything for him yet? Christmas is gonna be here before we know it."

"Not yet," Jeanne replied. "Have you?"

"Yup."

"What did you get him?"

"This book I found over where Oliver works. Its one of those big photo books, you know? It's like a visual history of motorcycles."

"Oh, good. You'll get him even more excited about it, and I can go around worrying more."

"Sorry," Claire laughed. "He really likes it, though. And besides, he rarely rides the thing."

"Yes, but he wants to take it somewhere far. He wants to travel on it like some vagabond man. You should see the way he talks about it. He thinks he's young again."

"Maybe he is," Claire smiled.

By Herself
Or, At Midnight

Even though it was very late Faye's eyes had adjusted enough for her room to become mostly visible. The window above her bed let in a faint light through the blinds, and it was there, where the glowing stripes marked the wall, that she repeatedly stared.

She thought about what her father said, how she didn't need to worry about dying. She was young and healthy and safe. But she couldn't help thinking about it. She couldn't stop the overwhelming thought that she and everyone she knew would someday die. How could she face another day of life knowing that it could all end at any time?

It was in between strands of childish contemplation that she really sensed what it meant to be mortal. Over and over she repeated the same words in her head.

I will die.

I will die.

I will die.

And then a feeling would form deep in her stomach, radiating up her chest and into her head. It was as if the realization that this would all end became a physical thing inside of her. She didn't just acknowledge that she would die. She felt it in every part of her being. She fully became the *I* within the words she chanted in her head, which meant she became the inevitable act of death as well.

Over time the issue changed from her own end to that of her family. She pictured her father dying and the world she would be left in without him. She saw her brother and sister dead—that is, she saw them simply not existing anymore, since she never thought about the morbid parts of death and didn't really know them anyway. She didn't know much more than that dying meant you just stopped living. She was still a child, an incredibly innocent and gentle one at that, and her young mind hadn't yet seen or acknowledged the more gruesome parts of life.

Faye began to grow tired thinking about dying. She was done with the whole idea of it. But she didn't want to go back to before she knew about death. She was proud of how smart she was, and she admitted that a smart person must very well know about death. So how was she to move on?

She decided the only smart way to handle this was to know as much as she could about death. She remembered when her teacher had told the class on their first day of school that learning about and understanding the world makes people stronger and better and kind.

It was with these thoughts that she made her plans. She would do what anyone else would do in order to learn, which was get a book about what she wanted to understand. Faye was quite confident in her ability to read. She was better than the rest of the kids in her class, though she thought it was probably because she wasn't so good at math. Nonetheless, she was able to read at a grade above the one she was in, and she was sure she could find a book that she could understand. She would ask her sister to take her to the library after school, and there she would find what she needed.

As Faye planned out the coming day in her head, her thoughts were able to escape the fascination that had kept her awake all night. She fell asleep into an empty dream that was nothing more than darkness.

December 24th, 1971
Or, Melt

Arthur thought of all the bad words he knew as he leaned against the cold metal of his father's car. He came up with seven in total. Three of them he had heard this morning.

The wind blew one last push before it died away. The air was still, and all that could be heard was the droning echo of silence against snow.

"Fuck," Arthur whispered, just to hear it out loud.

He pushed himself away from the car and kicked at the ground. Black snow painted the air. Frozen clumps of carbon and ice burst outward, slowing down as they grew apart until everything stopped.

The world was static.

Or was it Arthur's mind that was still?

The spotted sky reminded him of Domino. He wondered where his dog had run away to, if he was still alive at all. That was two years ago after all. He was probably dead.

The moment thawed, and the black that splattered the air fell with a wet thud against the street. Arthur stood amongst the landscape of white houses in white snow. He started watching his breath leave in soft clouds as he imagined what the day ahead would bring. In his mind he saw his family as they talked about things he didn't care about. He would try to be friendly with his cousins, but they were all in high school and wouldn't want to hang around him. The food would smell good but taste bad, and his mother would make him eat it nonetheless. He did at least look forward to getting a few presents, though he wasn't sure he would get anything that great.

The front door of Arthur's house opened and his father stepped out smoking a cigarette. He looked upset, though not as much as before. Arthur wondered if he should say anything. He decided to keep quiet and wait until he was spoken to.

"Here," his father said, reaching into his pocket. "Start the car." Arthur walked up to him, breathing in the smell of tobacco as his father handed him the keys. "Remember how?"

Arthur nodded yes and quickly walked his way back to the car. He unlocked the door and sat inside.

"Don't track in all that damn snow," his father shouted with a puff of smoke from his Pall Mall.

"Oh," Arthur muttered, quickly kicking his legs out of the car and knocking the snow from his shoes. He pulled himself back into the seat and put the keys in the ignition. He pressed a little on the gas as he turned the keys, and the car rumbled to life, breaking apart the quiet stillness that had blanketed the street. He revved the engine a few times before his father waved at him to get out.

"We leavin' soon?" Arthur asked.

"As soon as your mother's ready," his father answered, tossing his spent cigarette into the snow.

"Is Grandpa gonna be there?"

"He is. Though he won't be much for talking. He's not feeling well."

"Oh, alright."

"Listen, I'm sorry you had to hear me and your mother this morning. Adults argue sometimes, especially when they're married."

"Oh," Arthur replied.

"Is that all you ever say?" his father asked. Arthur stood silent, not knowing how to answer. "Anyway," his father continued, "someday you'll understand. You'll have a woman in your life, and you'll know what it means to love someone even though you're angry as hell at them."

Arthur turned to stare down the street just so he could look away from his father and the words that he spoke. He thought of Lisa, the last girl he had talked to. He had stared at her long blonde hair as she asked him what he was doing for Christmas vacation. He wasn't doing anything, and that's what he told her. As she turned away, uninterested in his answer, he imagined running his hand through her golden hair. It had made him feel strange inside, like he was going to melt away, and he again sensed that feeling as he stood in the snow of his front yard, thinking of both Lisa and the words that his father spoke.

"Let's go," his mother said, rushing out of the house.

"Yes, dear," his father replied, locking the door behind her.

The three of them got into the car. Arthur buckled himself in as he listened to the silent tension between his parents.

"How about some music?" asked his father, turning on the radio. Some sort of Christmas song crackled through. Trumpets and children singing about Santa Claus crowded the car. There was a moment of silence as the song ended. The radio quietly hummed.

"I don't want to listen to this," Arthur's mother spoke.

"It's Christmas time," his father said, "and—"

"And you'd probably rather spend it with that redhead of yours," she snapped.

"That's not true, and you know it."

"No, I don't know."

"Well, what do I have to do to prove it to you?"

The radio again came to life, playing some slow Bing Crosby song about the holidays. Arthur's parents went silent, and Arthur stared out the window of the backseat as houses passed by with Christmas lights brightly shining through the gray daylight.

Bing had just finished singing his chorus when Arthur's mother screamed out. His father slammed hard into the car's brakes, and they slid sideways across the icy road, the wheels beneath them squealing loudly against wet pavement. Arthur whipped around in his seat and banged his head against the glass. His mother kept yelling, and his father was spinning the steering wheel back and forth violently. Arthur couldn't see what was happening and never really knew.

The car finally came to a stop, and Bing's low voice still sang quietly on. Arthur sat himself up and rubbed the painful spot on his head.

"Arthur!" his mother cried. "Arthur! Are you okay?"

"Yeah," he answered, though his head did hurt. "I'm okay."

"That could have killed us," she said to herself in shock.

His father said nothing as he looked to his frightened wife. He reached his arms around her and pulled her in close. She wept within his arms, and as she did he stared over her shoulder into Arthur's eyes. Something in the way his father looked that very instant made Arthur understand love. He felt his father's thoughts, and he knew what they meant. His mother was right. Her husband did want to spend Christmas with a redhead. But it was love that kept him here instead. It was love that tore down his desires and replaced them with devotion.

Arthur didn't look away, not until his parents had let go of their embrace. His father grabbed the steering wheel, and again they drove down the snowy streets. Arthur felt the sore on his head and wondered about the woman he would someday love.

He Thought Of Nowhere
Or, His Escape

The Devil wept for everyone as he sat alone in Hell, leaning forward in his throne and staring sadly down at his hooved feet.

In his sad state he questioned the universe.

Why must life be so painful? Why must every living soul face the darkest depths of existence? And why must he, the king of Hell, be so evil? The Devil had seen the lowest lows, yet he knew nothing of the highest highs. He was one and the same with the most wicked of beings, but he hadn't the faintest glimpse of love.

He knew, however, through all of his lamenting, that his existence was necessary.

"No light without dark!" he roared out to himself, standing up and lifting his large fists into the air. "No hot without cold! No life without death!"

His rage ended abruptly, and his brow again tilted into a sad expression. His hands dropped slowly to his sides. His jagged lips frowned. "No good," he said miserably, falling back down into his lonely throne, "without evil."

Was virtue worth the complement of sin? Was the everlasting balance of love and hate merely a painful waste of time? Wouldn't it be better to simply never exist at all?

As Satan sat there in despair, deploring his necessary existence, a solitary teardrop fell from his eye. It caressed the rough crimson skin of his face, rolling down to the bottom of his large, piercing chin where it hung for an eternity.

He didn't want to be the King of Darkness. It's just that he was, had always been, and always would be. A stone must be a stone, and the sun must be the sun. To be something else is to not be at all. So how could he be anyone besides himself? If he were, then he would cease to exist. If he ceased to exist, then so would everyone else.

As he confronted his dilemma, another tear slowly fell across his jagged face. It joined with the other in eternity, and together they waited for the end. The more his torments troubled him, the more he formed drops of sorrow that collected on his chin. Eventually the weight became too heavy, even for the endlessness of time.

With one final thought of sadness a torrent fell from his face. The boundless teardrops, glowing in the infinite colors of melancholy, wept across Oliver's canvas. Brokenhearted hues intertwined themselves with the shades of truth and bliss, and there upon the painted form of his sorrow, Lucifer found the answer to why he, or anything at all, should exist.

It was beauty, in all of her infinite forms, as she swam amongst eternity. Through the lowest lows and the highest highs, caressing the universe with ecstasy, she painted Heaven with Hell, and Hell with Heaven. She needed no cause for her effect, no questions for her answers, no reason or purpose or meaning. She simply was. And she simply would always be.

Oliver lifted the dark green bottle to his lips and downed a heavy gulp of wine. It unpleasantly moved its way down his throat, though he enjoyed the feeling. His bottle was now empty, and his head had just slightly begun to stir. He gazed at his painting with drunken pleasure, not solely from the wine but from his own pride as well. Tomorrow he would despise his creation, but for now it was a masterpiece.

He put on his jacket and opened the door to his balcony. Taking out and lighting his last cigarette, he smoked away the cold night air. He thought of his painting inside, sitting there doing nothing besides being a painting. It wasn't making his life any better. It wasn't taking him to the places he wanted to go. It didn't make him become the man he wanted to be.

So why do it? Why do anything? Wouldn't he be content just living out his life as easily as possible? Wouldn't happiness come to him if he waited peacefully in the simple pleasures of life?

He thought of becoming a sort of recluse. He would forget all the troubles of being someone and go off to live a spiritual life of awareness and contemplation. He would need nothing at all, not even life itself.

But the wine in his veins fueled buried thoughts within his head, and out they flew into the open skies of his mind. He knew that he didn't belong within the solely virtuous realm of the holy. Instead, he was born to seek out the truth within both the vulgarities and the sanctities of life. It was within the whole scope of being human that he was destined to travel.

He wanted to create works of art that expressed his soul. He wanted to explore the depths of inner and outer space. He desired to caress the sensual and make love to the divine.

Couldn't he do all this without being someone? Couldn't he become who he wanted to be without becoming someone successful? Why did his dreams come hand in hand with fame and fortune? He wasn't even really sure what success was anyway. He knew that his life, and everyone's, really, was a one-way journey to an inevitable end. So what was to be had with it? What could a person do with their little plot of life that both pleased the one who lived within it and satisfied the one who would look back upon it from death?

His cigarette was half finished, and the nicotine began to dance with the wine in his head. He forgot the questions in his mind. He ignored the world that existed around him. Oliver closed his eyes and drifted away to a familiar spot within himself. It was a place that was never the same, a place he would often visit to escape the mundane. He had become accustomed to its chaos. The only quality that always returned was the indescribable nature of its being, its mysterious and perpetual sacredness. It was a fantastic realm within him that seemed more real than reality. He would fly, within the images of his mind, across landscapes made of countless impossibilities. Only when a certain idea would overtake his thoughts would his inner travels slow down into a place of faint coherence.

He was alone, as he always was in his dreams, in a land that was eternal. The universe inside his spirit was a solitary one, for he was everything within and without his being. The road that sat beside his apartment had become an endless path stretching on as far as he could see. The sky was gone, no longer even night. It was simply a void of pure black. Yet there was a glow upon the objects around him. The world was alight from the hidden radiance within everything.

He walked along the road as the familiar buildings and landscapes of his ordinary life became sparse. Eventually all was vacant, with the floating street beneath him being the only object within his abyss. The singular path led its way through nothing, and Oliver thought how wonderful it would be to take it anywhere he wished to go. A flash of images within his mind showed the endless possibilities of where he could travel and who he could become.

But a moment later, before his dreams could come into being, he was awoken to the reality that he had left behind. He shivered from the cold and took one last drag from his cigarette. He remembered his painting, and turning to look at it through the glass doors of his balcony, he thought it looked beautiful. He wasn't ashamed to believe so, and he wasn't ashamed to believe in himself.

Brightly Quiet
Or, Memorized

Faye stared at the multicolored rings floating gently upon a small sea of white. She pressed them down with her spoon and watched as they rose back to the surface, guided by some universal law that they weren't aware of but which they had to obey.

"Can you take me to the library, Claire?" she asked.

"They're closed," her sister answered. "It's Sunday."

"I know," Faye replied. "Can you take me tomorrow after school?"

"I suppose. Why?"

"I want some books to read."

"Imagine that. Books at the library."

"Thanks," Faye said, grabbing her bowl of cereal. She shook it and watched as the vibrant rings wobbled about in her milk. Lifting the bowl to her lips, she gulped down what was left. Afterwards she let out a groan from filling her stomach too full.

"That's what you get," Claire told her, eating small spoonfuls of cereal. The two sisters sat together on the floor beside the coffee table, watching cartoons that the both of them had seen countless times before. Faye tumbled to her side and stared sideways at the television.

"What kind of books do you want?" Claire asked.

Faye wondered how to answer. Did she want to tell her sister that she needed a book about dying? For some reason she felt embarrassed about it. She thought she was strange for thinking about death. At her age she should be reading books about magic and animals and all sorts of things like that.

"Hello?" Claire said, waving her hand at Faye.

"I dunno!" Faye yelled, climbing up onto the sofa beside her. She stuffed her face in between the cushions and breathed in the smell of old fabric and crumbs from food long ago.

"Don't do that," Claire told her, pulling on the back of her sister's shirt. "It's nasty in there." Faye lifted herself out of the cushions and sat silently watching the television. She heard her dad walk by, though he didn't stop to say anything. She listened as he walked into the hallway and up the stairs to his bedroom.

The December morning sun was shining brightly through the windows. It seemed to hit every object in just the perfect way, and a slight halo burned around everything it touched. The brightness of it all made Faye feel happy.

"You are stupid!" she yelled out, mirroring from memory what was being said on the cartoon she watched.

"And don't forget! You are stupid!" Claire yelled out quickly after, smiling alongside her sister. The two of them sat content, watching whatever the television showed them.

"What're we doing today?" Faye asked as an oddly placed commercial for health insurance came on. Her sister said nothing, shrugging her shoulders for an answer while still staring at the TV. Faye didn't like her sister's response, so she scooted herself across the sofa and poked her on the cheek. "What're we doing?" she asked again.

"Nothing!" Claire yelled, pushing her sister away and standing up. "Sitting around until it's tomorrow." She took her empty bowl of cereal and walked out of the room. Faye sat alone on the sofa, staring out of the window at the corner of blue sky that she was just barely able to see. She had mostly forgotten about her problem of death, and her thoughts drifted back into a simple state that wanted nothing other than to be happy. Life was, for the moment, uncomplicated. She was an innocent child again, and all there was to do was live.

Her father returned from upstairs. He sat beside her on the couch and wrapped his large, warm arms around her.

"How about going to Grandma and Grandpa's for lunch?" he asked, pinching at her small toes and squeezing them. She laughed and squirmed her feet away.

"Okay," she said, climbing down his leg and grasping her small hands around his large feet. She poked and prodded at his toes until his feet lifted from the floor, and as they did she tickled the bottoms of them. He laughed and pulled his legs up, tucking them under his body. "Hey!" she yelled out, scrambling up the couch and pulling at his legs.

"Grandma made your favorite," he said, grabbing Faye and holding her down on the sofa. "Apple pie."

He tickled her sides and she laughed and screamed and wriggled about. She was excited to go to her grandparents'. She liked the way her grandpa talked. She didn't understand much of what he said, but the way he said it in his deep soft voice made her feel happy. And her grandma always gave her something sweet she baked herself, like apple pie or chocolate brownies.

Faye did think their house smelled funny, though not really bad. It smelled like nothing else she had ever smelled, so she couldn't really describe it, other than that it smelled like her grandparents' house. She also thought it was strange to watch her grandpa from far away, when he didn't know she was watching. Most of the time he looked happy, but every so often his lips would gently frown and his eyes would look sad as he seemed to stare at nothing. Faye was afraid to ask him what was wrong, so she would turn and walk away, pretending she didn't see him.

Her father patted her on the head and told her to get ready.

"It's almost over," she told him, referring to the cartoon on TV, which had just come back on. He walked away, and Faye could hear him talking to Claire in the other room. A cloud passed by outside, turning the bright room dull for just a moment. Faye didn't notice the change as she sat staring at the cartoon she had memorized by heart.

The Earth Is Made Of You
Or, Teenage Cosmos

It was too early for Claire to think right. Her head was full of noise and nothing, neither of which allowed her to pay much attention in class. She didn't listen to her teacher as he scribbled words on the chalkboard and talked about layers of the earth.

Claire wrote half-legible notes regarding geology, usually just a jotted word with a minimal and careless definition alongside it. More of her attention was spent on the borders of her paper, where she would doodle whatever came to her drifting thoughts. Her pen traced out shapes that spun in eddies of blue ink, flowing along muddled paths until an object would form, one which usually hinted at what she was supposed to be learning. Chunks of rock fell along her pen marks, colliding against pools of lava and tumbling down slabs of tectonic plates. Her finest drawing, she thought, was a cake with icing that resembled Earth. It had a large piece cut away, revealing that it was a layer cake with vanilla icing crust, red velvet mantle, and a butter cream core. The candles on top were melting down themselves and onto the surface, and she thought for a moment of the symbolic nature of her drawing. Wasn't it true that Earth was doomed to someday melt away, smothering itself in suicidal celebration? Weren't the little creatures living upon it the candle makers that brought about that fatal birthday?

She thought about it for a while and realized that people weren't the only possible cause for Earth's end. Everything has its dying day, and the earth would eventually die no matter what people had done to it. If humans do happen to make the end occur, then they will have merely sped up the process.

Her teacher said something she didn't listen to, and the class began to rustle their papers and close their books. She sat half aware, leaving behind her apocalyptic musings and trying to awaken herself to life at school.

It wasn't that Claire disliked learning. She actually was madly in love with it. And it wasn't that she was a bad student, acting out against those who said they aimed to teach her the truth. She was, in fact, a very good student. She had good grades, was often involved in extracurricular activities, and was on good terms with most of her fellow classmates.

She was, however, tired of it all.

She already knew most of what she was taught, and her time in school seemed like a waste of life. Couldn't she do more if she were free to discover herself outside of these thick brick walls? She felt like she was adrift in a sea of automation. Every person around her seemed to do what teenagers were supposed to do and nothing else. They studied, didn't study, dated, didn't date, talked, didn't talk, and most of all they acted like they were the center of the universe, like they were somebody. Her friends swam about their little identities, being someone they thought they ought to be, even if it meant being someone they didn't really like. She knew, though, that none of them, herself included, understood what they wanted to be. They were too young, too naïve, too ignorant to really know anything at all.

It was thoughts like these that made her feel old even though she was only eighteen. And the fact that she was eighteen yet only a junior made her feel stunted in life. For some reason or other Claire started school a year later than most kids, and for that she was a year older than all the other students in her class. This displacement always seemed to put her at a slight advantage because she was naturally more developed than the others, but at the same time it was a subtle bane to her life, holding her back from the not-so-distant future in which she was meant to live.

Claire silently laughed at herself for being who she was and for being who she was in such a teenage way. But wasn't she getting older all the time? Yes, she was young now, but that wouldn't last. She conclusively realized that she would someday either be eighty years old or dead, and she wanted to live her life before one of those two realities came into being.

Her apathy of that morning won over her thoughts before she could decide on what to do, and she quickly stopped caring about who she ought to be. She instead focused on merely staying awake in class. She had been up late last night, sitting on the Internet and doing mostly nothing at all. The weekend had been entirely uneventful, as was most of her life, it seemed. She had spent yesterday at her grandparents, watching television and eating the countless desserts her grandmother made. Now it was Monday morning, and she had no drive to do anything at all.

The bell rang, releasing the class and stirring Claire awake. She walked with the others out of the room and into the hallway. All around her people were talking, and all the while she was lost inside herself as she hurriedly moved along. She walked to her locker, traded out her geology book for her English one, and headed to her next class. There she sat at her desk and waited. After a moment, Megan and Amy walked in together, sitting beside her.

"Claire," Amy said, pulling stuff out of her bag, "we really need your help."

"Sure," she answered. "With what?"

"We're making postcards to send to the families of the bombing victims," Megan said, handing Claire a notebook with ideas written all over the page, "and we're gonna collect money to donate too. Do you think you could make signs to hang up around school?"

"Oh, sure, of course," she replied.

She thought about the incident. Someone had bombed a subway station in California, and it just so happened that a team of high school basketball players were right there at the time, along with the cheerleaders and coaches and a few of the parents. They were traveling on some trip together across the state to a tournament, and they had the day free to spend visiting some of the sights. Their trip ended there in the subway. Every one of them died, along with the dozens of others that were in the station. They hadn't discovered who did it yet, though everyone seemed to think it was terrorists of some sort. The politics of it were where she began to lose interest. She was saddened for what had happened, and she felt awful for the victims and their families, but as soon as the news began to mention the various groups and governments possibly involved she drifted away from the incident.

"I just can't believe someone would do that," Megan said, shaking her head. "I mean, to kill that many people," she shook her head even more, raising her arms into the air, "to kill anyone at all!"

"It's pretty bad," Amy said, "and that's why we need to help."

Claire nodded in agreement and scanned through the notes she had been given. She wondered what it would feel like to be blown up. She shuddered at the thought of it, imagining her skin melting and her limbs popping off as her head ripped away from her body.

The subject of exploding pushed her deeper into a sad lethargy. She was tired of this world, and yet all she had ever known and experienced was her little American way of living. How could she possibly stand up to a real life in the real world? Maybe she was better off drifting along in her clueless teenage sea, worrying about nothing important and doing nothing important. Maybe she should be grateful to have the opportunity to be no one at all.

She saw in her head large candles as they melted across the earth. No one cared enough to blow them out. Everyone made their wishes, but they all held their breath.

The bell rang and class began.

Claire's head was full of noise and nothing. She didn't listen to her teacher as he scribbled words on the wall, talking about the layers of meaning in the story they had read.

The Sound Of Us
Or, Noise

The day was heavy, and the sky was gray. Oliver gazed out of his window, disheartened by the dullness of the world. He thought of all the people, all the noise, and all the pointless things that were happening everywhere. He saw himself in the middle of it, unable to escape, glued together by some hidden force. He was just another molecule amongst all the other boring molecules, and everyone was busy, oh so busy, doing nothing at all.

A solitary patch of blue sky drifted through the clouds as if it were taunting Oliver and his life. It teased his thoughts and told him that there was so much more than what he had. A hidden paradise lived on above him, veiled by the clouds of his reality, too obscured for his eyes to see, too distant for his arms to embrace.

He criticized himself for being so cynical. His life wasn't that bad. He knew that existence had much to offer, and that he would have to work hard for what he wanted to find. Most of his life he had searched for his dreams with a mask of idle despair to guide him, but only as of late, and a little more every day, he learned that the only way to find truth was to fully open his eyes and look for it.

Oliver appreciated his fortune of a peaceful life, one without starvation or violence or the overwhelming pain that so many other people had to face. He lived during an era when mankind was at its greatest potential for greed and hate, and every day he confronted a world that seemed to feed those dark human desires. There were people killing people, companies destroying the earth, governments feeding lies to the masses, and idiotic societies swallowing the countless distractions that soften their minds and dissolve their hearts.

He, however, lived an easygoing life amongst it all, and it often troubled him to think about this fact. He believed that only through great difficulty could he find that hidden treasure his soul searched for. How could he ever discover it within his easy middle-class American life? How could his spirit climb its heights and sound its depths if he was stranded in the middle of the flat, mundane, convenient world of this modern insincerity?

He sometimes wondered if what he was looking for might be right in front of him, dancing amongst the avaricious hollowness. Or maybe even right inside of him, connected to the deepest parts of his being. Perhaps what he sought was the easiest thing in the universe to see, even amidst the shallow puddles of ordinary life. He just had to let go of the questions in order to understand the answer.

Even if he pushed aside his personal troubles, a looming problem remained. Why should he have such a peaceful life when so many others were in anguish? Who was he to brood about some spiritual problem when his life was so easy and free of pain? And what could he do to fix the world that was littered with so much turmoil?

He had heard countless times before that every change begins with one person, but it seemed impossible to him that he could transform this enormous planet full of suffering. There were too many problems and too many people and too many forces working against him. So he lived with the weight of knowing he did nothing. In his mind he believed he took from the world and gave nothing back. The heaviness grew upon his conscience every day because deep down he knew his inaction was due to laziness and not futility.

Oliver finished his coffee just as the spot of blue sky drifted out of sight. He got ready for the day ahead and left his apartment behind to face the world that he had been contemplating all morning. His preconceived notion that the day would be a bleak one made it so, and every experience seemed to him to be dismal. As he approached his car he felt a sense self-loathing build within him. Why should the world suffer so he could move about quickly and comfortably? If he was sincere about saving the earth he should walk everywhere and refuse to drive.

Nevertheless, he got inside his car and started it, where he sat waiting for the engine to warm up, listening to its heavy hum as it painfully came to life.

After the complex assembly of mechanics and chemistry awoke from its cold slumber, Oliver directed it down the copious roads of concrete that sprawled across the Earth. He moved his heavy machine alongside countless other heavy machines that carried their passengers wherever they wished to go, so long as they could afford to do so. One could hardly call this transportation a convenience, however, due to the sheer amount of hassle that went into obtaining and operating these demanding vehicles. After facing the heaps of bureaucracy to be lawfully able to drive, people had to work away their lives just to afford a proper automobile. Most couldn't even do that, so they signed away their days to banks who lent them the money. Once a person possessed a vehicle they had to feed it gasoline, a liquid that came from deep within the earth. It was a resource that slowly polluted the landscape and gave power to people that shouldn't have it. Even after the automobiles were fed they lived ruinous lives that made them frequently break down. The owners had to pay more money, which in reality meant more of their time, in order to get them fixed.

Oliver sat facing one of the most tedious aspects of driving a car, which was the mind-numbing experience of ceaseless traffic. It was a situation that was inevitable for those that drove an automobile, and it degraded away at the passengers' spirits as they sat waiting away their lives. For Oliver it was even worse, because driving brought out the most selfish parts of a deep and voracious anger. He swore at those who got in his way and ridiculed those who he thought drove stupidly. He was aware of himself the entire time, but he couldn't seem to change.

Oliver pulled into a parking spot at one of the department store in town. He needed to buy some pants because one of his three pairs finally ripped apart too much for him to wear. He hated buying new clothes. He didn't want to support companies that paid people across the world very little to work all day. He also hated buying new clothes because he ashamedly felt excited at getting them, even though he despised the idea of it. After reading *Walden* a few years back he swore to give up, among other things, wearing impressive clothing. He would only dress in what was essential. This didn't last long, though, as he slowly acquired more and more new clothes over time. All that remained was his belief in avoiding new outfits, not the actual act of doing so, which put him in a state of self-disgust whenever he went shopping.

He walked in through the automatic doors and was instantly besieged by the numerous ads that covered the store. Hanging from the ceiling were giant, happy pictures of happy people doing happy things with the happy stuff they happily bought. On the walls were teenage girls dressed in skintight clothes, posing like softcore porn stars. They stuck their asses out at the people that walked by and pouted their bright red lips at those who stared.

Oliver walked as straight as possible to the men's clothing section, trying to avoid seeing the models on the walls, though his eyes often glanced in their direction. Suddenly he was staring at rows upon rows of pants, and above them were muscular men with stupid-looking haircuts. They all stood around nonchalantly in their brand new jeans.

Noise blasted through the speakers above. It was what many people called music, though Oliver didn't believe so. In fact, he thought of it as the opposite of music. It was the antithesis of beauty, of melody, of rhythm. It was waves of tedious noise blasted against a repetitive and simple drumming sound. All of this was topped by the idiotic and painfully annoying vocals of someone singing into a computer. The lyrics were an ode to being forever young and stupid, which to Oliver seemed to be the general goal of mankind.

He found some pants that seemed to fit and walked to the checkout, trying again to avoid looking at the girls plastered on the wall and failing to do so. When he got to the register he waited in line until it was his turn to pay. As he pulled his credit card out of his wallet, he tried to remember a day that went by without him spending any money. As the cashier handed him his receipt, he realized he couldn't remember such a day. This threw him into deep thought as he walked to his car. What kind of world did he live in? Had everything been turned into a business? Was the meaning of life to be bought and sold?

He opened the door to his car and sat down in despair. Was he no different from everyone else? Was his life story one of economy? Were his thoughts and his actions shaped by the value of their profits? And most importantly, would he do anything to change the way he lived?

His answer was yes. Even more so, he wanted to change the world and not just himself. Sitting there in the parking lot of the place that stood for all that he was vowing against, he swore to try as hard as he could to leave the business of life behind and to live solely for the act of living, not for the profits to be gained.

He pulled out of the parking lot and drove, not thinking of driving at all but somehow getting to his destination safely. Another day of work was ahead of him, though he greeted it with high spirits. He had defeated his earlier pessimism, and he would now drift through the day, dreaming of what he would do with his life.

By tomorrow his ideas would soften, and most of them would melt away, but a certain trace of them would remain, lingering in his being and changing who he was.

December 24th, 1978
Or, Everything Goes

"I can't fucking stand it," Larry said, exhaling a cloud of smoke. Arthur nodded in agreement and followed with his own puff of gray. Larry continued ranting. "I mean, who the hell actually likes the shit? It's trash. Absolute trash, man."

"Everyone likes it," Arthur replied, leaning his head against the brick wall behind him.

"Yeah, fucking everyone," Larry laughed. "I don't get it. Nobody actually feels what they're singing about. All sorts of love and heartbreak and dancing and sunshine fucking rainbows. It's shit, man."

"If I hear the Bee Gees one more time I'll kill myself," Arthur said with a wide smile.

"Exactly. One more fucking time. And you know what? You will hear them one more fucking time. You'll hear all this shit a hundred more times."

"That's life, man. People make bad art. People make all sorts of bad shit. They always have and always will."

"I suppose. But this stuff is really bad," Larry said after taking a heavy drag from his cigarette.

"Every generation makes the worst stuff until the next generation comes along." Arthur said, standing up and walking to the side of the patio. "And people will always swallow it, even if it is shit. But you know, with the worst comes the best. There's some good stuff out there."

"The good stuff is dead, man."

"And the good stuff will be born again."

"Yeah, yeah," Larry replied. "Listen, what're you doing tonight?"

"What do you mean what am I doing tonight?" Arthur asked, tossing his spent cigarette into the frozen lawn. "It's goddamn Christmas Eve, man. I'll be with my family."

"I'm just saying," Larry urged, "my brother's getting some beer for me tonight. I'm betting I could get the Kersey girls over here too. Twins and beer!"

"I'm betting the Kersey girls are gonna be with their family too, ya know. How 'bout next week or something?"

"I ain't got shit to do tonight, so tonight I'm getting fucked up. My mom's half a Jew and my dad doesn't give a damn about anything."

"You can come to my family's Christmas. They won't mind. There'll be food and stuff."

"Don't give me that shit. I'm no poor and abused child. I'm just raised by two stiffs. No holidays, no birthdays, no smiles, no nothing, besides a roof over my head and food on the table. My god, I don't know how me and my brother can even function."

"Well, whatever you do, take it easy. And if you do get the Kerseys over here, give 'em a nice hello from me." Arthur said, grabbing his denim coat and grinning at Larry.

"You leavin'?" Larry asked from the steps where he sat.

"Christmas Eve, remember?"

"Yeah, yeah. Well, take it easy."

"Yup," Arthur said, walking out into the crisp, dead grass and waving behind to his friend. He lifted his collar up and stuck his hands into the warm, wool-lined pockets of his coat. He moved onto broken sidewalks that ran alongside the quiet suburban street. His feet left shallow imprints in the thin layer of snow that had fallen earlier that morning. Breathing in and out the cold air, Arthur wondered to himself what his future would be like. Would he find a woman to love? Would he have kids? Would he become someone important, or become no one at all? And did any of it matter? What if there was no reason to be successful, no reason to fall in love, aside from his own desires?

He imagined what the world would be like and if the music would get any better. What if everything just kept getting worse? Our art would become less and less beautiful, our wars would become more and more violent, our minds would decay away, and our lives would vanish into a hazy cloud of failure.

His questions seemed meaningless compared to the life playing out in front of him. He was about to graduate from high school and go into college. The weight of success was tossed upon his shoulders by people other than himself. He forced himself forward with becoming somebody even though he felt he was already somebody enough.

Arthur walked past the strip mall with all its closed stores, pass the empty auto shop and the vacant library and school, and down the streets lined with houses plastered in bright Christmas lights. He knew he would soon be home and would soon be greeted by his parents.

They hadn't talked much lately. Arthur often turned aloof when they were around. And he noticed that his father and mother rarely said more than a few words to each other. It had become a quiet house, and Arthur was waiting for the silence to erupt. It wasn't that that there was anger amongst them. In fact, he felt a strange sort of love flowing through the soundless home. But he knew that beneath it all there were restless thoughts that wanted to come out. They wanted to scream to the others that they were there and that this is how they felt.

Arthur wondered if he would be the one to burst.

He reached his front door and opened it to the smell of his mother's cooking. There was something sweet in the air, like blueberries or cherries, and hidden behind the sweetness was the savory smell of rosemary and thyme and other herbs that he didn't know.

His father was in the living room watching TV. A holiday show was on, and Arthur could make out the sound of children singing Christmas songs against a messy backdrop of violins.

He crept quietly to his room and fell upon his bed, where he pressed his face into his pillow and breathed in and out the warm air that never traveled far from his lungs.

No souls would speak today. Maybe none ever would.

Perhaps the whole world would slowly sink into loud silence.

And So It Has Been Written
Or, The Voice Of Distant Others

Faye's fingers typed DEATH with ease. It was her head that seemed to have trouble, and she hesitated a moment before pressing enter. Should she be looking up something like this? What if someone saw her? And what if she found something she didn't want to see? Death was, after all, something mostly hidden from her. It was as if those older than her knew that it was something bad, something that should be kept from the eyes of children.

But she couldn't resist the urge to know what she didn't know. She pressed the enter key and waited. A long list of book names fell across the screen, and along with them the numbers that told where they belonged in the library. Faye let out a small sigh. She had only just memorized where things were in the children's section, and now she had to face the much larger, and much darker, adult's section.

She took one of the little yellow pencils that sat in a box beside the computer, and she slowly wrote down the numbers of the first few books on the list. Afterwards she walked her way across the library, passing her sister, who was wandering along the aisles of movies and music. Faye headed in the direction of the first number on her list, or at least where she thought that number might be. Row by row she passed tall shelves of books, more than she had ever seen before, and she glanced at the large black and white numbers that were posted on the ends of them. Though she felt a little lost, she also felt excited and happy. She was comfortable around books, even ones that she couldn't understand, and the worlds inside of them pleased her mind and let her imagination explore. She also loved the way they smelled. It was a sort of dusty scent that reminded her of a past she never had.

Faye finally found the aisle that she was looking for. Heading down the row of books, Faye ran her fingers along the varied spines, feeling the rough canvas of books from long ago beside the smooth plastic ones from today. Her eyes gazed upon the countless different colors and words that sat all around her, and she had to focus hard to keep her attention on finding what she was looking for. Just as she neared the end of the long bookshelf she found the book that she sought.

The Death Of Failure: Financial Achievement Amid Profit Loss

Faye pulled the book from the shelf and stared at its bright red cover. She thought about its title, which was spelled out in large golden letters, and managed to realize that it wasn't what she was looking for. She wasn't concerned about money since she only had four dollars of her own, and she didn't really have much to fail at besides doing well in school. Maybe when she was older, she thought, she could use a book like that. Though she wasn't fond to the idea of having money since it seemed that it would give her something to fail at.

She walked her way to where the next book would be. After a few minutes of searching she found it, or rather, where it was supposed to be. All that sat in its spot was an emptiness between two books.

Faye felt discouraged at her two attempts so far. She wished she had studied the list a little more, but she was worried someone would see her looking up books about death. Now she was adrift in the library with a little card covered in numbers with no names beside them.

She decided to take a break from her search and simply roam about. Moving down the aisles with no particular goal aside from finding something interesting, she stared at the numerous book titles upon the shelves, many of which she couldn't really understand. Every so often she would stop when something caught her eye. Usually it was a certain color or picture, and the book itself would do little to amuse her.

Modern Politics: A Human's View grabbed her attention because of its vibrant letters, each one of which was colored with a different country's flag. But the inside was disappointingly boring, and the few pictures it had were only of really rich people or really poor people, neither of which she had ever actually seen before. And as far as politics went she had absolutely no concern over what happened so long as people weren't getting hurt. And the earth itself had to be taken care of too, which from her small amount of time upon it was something she had discovered to be often forgotten.

You, Me, And Social Media seemed interesting at first. Its cover was reflective like a mirror, and Faye stared at herself, giggling as she twisted her face into strange shapes by bending the book around. Again, however, the inside was boring. She slowly read some of the words, but they didn't mean much to her. She didn't belong to any social media, a term that she had just discovered within the book, though she already knew of them. Her dad only let her on the Internet every so often to study for school, or, if she was lucky, to play games. And he only let her when he was around. Her sister was online all the time, though, and most of the time she was on her favorite websites where she could share stuff about herself with lots of other people. Faye would sit near and watch her sister type away, and Claire would often ignore the fact that she was there. She would put pictures of herself up on the Internet, which she had taken with her cellphone, and talk to her friends about whatever it was they talked about. To Faye this seemed as boring as the book that was written about it. She liked to play games and learn about the world, but sitting on a computer just so you could talk about yourself seemed kind of dumb.

Faye decided to continue searching for her books, especially since she had wasted time and was afraid her sister would come along looking for her at any moment. She had gotten used to this section of the library pretty quickly, and she checked the next number on the list, walking to where it would be. She found it sitting high upon the shelf, and she had to pull up a stool so she could reach it. Balancing herself so she could grab the book without falling, she stretched her arm as high as she could and was barely able to pull the book away. She stepped down, and, before even reading the title, stood eagerly hoping that it was a good book. She didn't want to have to put back. She wasn't even sure if she could.

Transience Within: Our Views On Death sat in Faye's hands. She didn't understand what the first word meant, but from the picture on the cover she could tell it was a book about the kind of death she wanted to understand. In the center was a brightly colored, elaborate skull, which Faye thought was actually kind of pretty, and from behind it shot out rays of light that radiated across the otherwise black cover.

Would this book tell her what she wanted to know or not? Either way it would have to do. She was running out of time, and she knew her sister was probably looking for her.

She walked her way back to the children's section, and she found the familiar, bright room comforting. She had explored enough of the adult world, and for now she was glad to be back where she belonged. Still, she was quite proud of her journey into the world of grown-up ideas, and she was exhilarated by the thought that she would someday call that place home.

Faye grabbed the small pile of books she had set aside. She didn't really want them, but she couldn't possible check out her one book about death. What would her sister think? And what about the librarian?

Just then Claire surprised her, walking out from behind a display of books about Santa Claus. She had a grin on her face, and Faye wondered how long she had been standing there.

"You ready to go?" Claire asked, setting a big blue book about the birth of Jesus back onto the display.

"Yeah," Faye replied, shuffling the books around in her hands.

"Give me those," her sister said. "I'll check everything out, and we can leave." Faye handed the pile of books to her sister and hoped that she wouldn't care to look at them. Claire took them and turned away to head to the counter. "So what did ya get?" she asked.

"Some books," Faye answered, following.

"What kind of books?" Claire asked, giving Faye a funny look.

Faye pretended not to hear her question. She used this tactic a lot, knowing that people expected her to not pay attention since she was so young.

The two of them reached the front desk, and Claire placed all of their books onto the counter. Faye was anxiously wishing in her head that her sister wouldn't see the big black book about death and that the lady at the desk would think that it was for Claire. Apparently her wish came true because nobody made any comments about it.

The two sisters quietly left the library behind to head out into the cold evening snow. They walked home through the calm dusk of winter. The sun was just beginning to hide behind the snowy horizon. Claire never said a word the whole way home, but Faye didn't mind. She liked to listen to the snow crunching beneath her boots.

Within a couple of minutes they were home. Faye quickly tore off her winter clothes, which were wet from melted snow, and she raced to the bag of books they had brought back from the library. She pulled out all of the children's books and hid the large black book beneath them. She scrambled up the steps, nearly tripping from her anxiety, and ran to her room. Her father yelled something from downstairs, though she couldn't quite hear him. She tossed the books down upon her bed and placed the book about death beneath her pillow.

Her father yelled again, and this time she understood him. She turned to run downstairs for dinner, but as she did she glimpsed a book on her bed that didn't look familiar. It was a children's book for sure. It was both tall and wide, but pretty thin. On the cover was a sad looking kid holding the hand of someone taller than the cover could show. She picked it up and read the title.

Where Life Goes

Faye was confused. She didn't remember grabbing it at the library. How did she end up with it? Was it someone else's? She knew it wasn't something her sister would read. And it seemed awfully relevant to what she wanted.

Her father yelled again, and Faye tossed the book back down on the bed. She would have to think about it later. For now life was calling her, and death would have to wait.

So On And So Forth
Or, Young Decisions

"So what do you think about it?" Amy asked.

"I think you need to just let him know," Megan answered.

"Yeah, you should," Claire added.

"But, I mean, what about his feelings?" Amy continued. "I don't want to hurt him. I do still love him."

"You can't love him and Brad both," Megan teased.

"Yeah, she can," Claire said.

"What?"

"Why can't someone be in love with more than one person? Don't you think there's enough room inside us to love a lot of people?"

"Don't give me your hippie shit, Claire." Megan laughed.

"I'm serious. It seems a little strange to me that we have to love one person when we could love so many more."

"It wouldn't really be love," Amy cut in. "It's more like a crush when it's shared around. I think true love only loves one person."

"Well, then do you love Brad or Justin?" Megan asked. Amy sat quiet, seemingly thinking about the answer. Claire fell back onto the shag rug beneath her. The sound of thin music coming from Amy's cellphone lulled her away for a moment as she stared at the muted television and the commercials that played across its screen.

"Brad," Amy finally answered.

"Ha!" Megan shouted, slapping her hands down onto the blue shag rug. Claire quickly sat up.

"Are you sure?" she asked Amy, who shook her head yes.

"I'm ready to move on," she answered. "Justin isn't the one." She paused. "Brad probably isn't either," she said, smiling halfheartedly. "I mean, in a few years we'll all be going away to college anyway. So I need to be free, really. Maybe I don't love either of them."

"Oh boy," Megan said, shaking her head. "Somebody get this girl a drink."

"Or maybe you love both of them!" Claire laughed, tossing a pillow at Amy. Megan reached past the two of them and grabbed the remote control, unmuting the television.

"Turn the music off," she told Amy, who was laughing and swinging a pillow at Claire. Amy grabbed her phone and stopped the high-pitched music coming from it. The room was now filled with the noise of television. A show about a wild pop star was on, and clips of interviews were being played.

"I don't wanna watch this crap," Claire said, tossing her body back down onto the baby blue rug.

"Stop it," Megan replied. "We're just watching this until your damn vampire show comes on. Besides, I think it's interesting. I mean, this guy had everything, then he threw it all away, and then he somehow came back again. Now look at him! He's the best singer out there."

Claire thought he was rather lame, but kept quiet because she didn't feel like talking about it. She pulled out her cellphone and mindlessly rummaged through her staple websites, which she visited whenever possible. Nobody had said anything to her, and nothing had happened. That was usually the case, but she had to check them nonetheless.

Her thumbs scrolled across her phone while she sprawled upon the floor, thinking about herself and who she wanted to be. The questions in her mind turned outwards when she began to wonder who she would someday love.

Did she really believe you could love more than one person? She pictured herself with two lovers whom she loved equally. One was light-skinned, blonde, and rugged looking. The other was tall, dark, and, of course, handsome, but he had a strange sort of oddness to him that made him peculiarly attractive. Each of them had two lovers as well, and their lovers had lovers who had lovers with lovers. And so on and so forth until everyone loved each other.

Claire felt a little silly for daydreaming about a planet full of attractive people loving each other freely, and she admitted it was a little farfetched. But she did wonder why it couldn't happen. It seemed so perfect, and why should life be anything but perfect?

Her friends were talking about the pop star on television, and Claire was drifting further and further away into her thoughts. She gently criticized her friends for being so stereotypically teenage-like, but her criticism slowly turned its focus inward. She wasn't much different from them. Aside from being a little more open-minded, she was just another teenager. She felt trapped in this juvenile state. If she tried harder at being someone she would consequentially become more of a teenager, since that's what teenagers do. But if she tried less at being someone she would fall into the pit of normalcy. Would she just have to ride out the wave of teenage life, waiting until the time when she could finally be someone without being someone?

Her questions turned confusing, and her thoughts became tired of themselves. She was fed up with living inside her head. She wanted to change her life. She couldn't be Claire anymore, or at least the Claire that she had been up to now. Even if it made her more of a teenager she was going live her life how she wanted to.

"Your show's coming on," Megan said, pulling Claire away from her self-examination. She sat up and let her resolution drift away. She had waited a week for this episode, and she needed to know what happened. Her transformation could wait. Though she did feel a little sorry for herself, as if she had found freedom but returned willingly to captivity.

A handsome vampire dressed in black walked onto the TV screen, grinning just enough to let his fangs show. His red eyes glanced at Claire. She wondered whom he loved, and she forgot about herself.

Bound
Or, You've Come A Long Way

"Home sweet home," Mike said, turning away from the window and staring across the room. He wore a large smile that pressed his cheeks upwards against his half-shut red eyes. He looked to Oliver. "I know nothing is permanent. Everything is fleeting. Even the most beautiful, significant, sincere, and loving things will disappear. But that doesn't make them any less beautiful, significant, sincere, and loving." He shook his head in disbelief. "Look at what I've been given. Or rather, what I somehow got. Or rather, rather, what I am. This home. This life. This family. Hell, even you! I'm even you! I'm everything!"

"Word," Oliver replied, somewhat understanding him, yet somewhat not. He knew what Mike was talking about, and wanted to believe it, but he was more inclined to side with the negative aspect of Mike's rambling. Everything dies.

"What about you, man?" Mike asked before taking a long drag from the nearly finished spliff in his hand. He blew out a cloud of smoke and passed it to Oliver. "What do you think?"

"I don't think much," Oliver answered. He took a small hit and offered the spliff back to Mike.

"No thanks," he replied, shaking his hand. "I'm good."

Oliver finished it off alone as he and Mike sat listening to the music that played across the room. Blue moonlight glistening off the snow outside cast itself through the window beside Mike, mixing with the soft, warm light of two small lamps glowing in the opposite corner of the room. The smoky atmosphere calmed Oliver, and the company of his friend helped to ease the anxiety that easily arose when he was high. Often times his thoughts would build upon themselves in heaps of paranoia. Improbable punishments by some god within his mind seemed to become realities that lurked behind every corner, and his inner self would turn into some pathetic being, frail and afraid of everything. Lately, though, he had slowly overcome that weakness, partly because he'd become more courageous in his thoughts and actions, and partly because he simply stopped caring about the bad things that could happen to him. He had accepted that eventually something awful would occur and that there was no point in dreading the inevitable. That was life. This recognition didn't bring him an enlightened joy. It merely gave him an indifferent bravery to the endless possibilities of his demise.

"What're you thinking?" Mike asked.

"What?" Oliver asked back.

"What're you thinking?" Mike repeated.

"Nothing."

"No way, man. You've been sitting there thinking for the last five minutes. I watched you."

"Five minutes?"

"Five minutes."

"Oh, well, I'm not sure what I was thinking about. Life I guess. Ya, know?"

"Yeah, I know. It's pretty crazy existing."

"Yeah."

"I mean, just what the hell is reality anyway?" Mike asked, looking back out of the window. "Is it this? I has to be, right?"

"I dunno if it has to be," Oliver answered, "but it seems to be the only thing we could logically call reality. This is the only thing we know. Our own life is the only thing we can understand, the only thing we can call real. Yet even then we can only say it with a tinge of certainty. Can we really trust our senses to tell us the truth?"

"To be honest," Mike said, standing from his seat and walking to his desk, "I'm not sure I could even define reality. Just what is it?"

"Something that's real," Oliver said, turning his chair to face Mike, who was beginning to mess with the electronics piled upon his desk.

"Exactly," Mike said as the hum of his equipment came to life. "So then define real."

"Something that's true. Something that genuinely exists."

"Bah," Mike scoffed, waving his hand in the air, "Words don't mean a thing. We're getting lost. If there is a reality its not in the names that we give it. It just is."

"If there is a reality," Oliver repeated quietly, trailing off into thoughts of imagination.

Mike shuffled around, flipping switches and turning knobs. Wires swam across his desk, connecting old electronics to each other. Children's toys were ripped open, their insides altered by his electrical know-how. A Game Boy, its screen glowing green, was transformed into a musical instrument and connected to his computer. At his feet were stomp boxes of every sort, able to delay and crunch and reverberate his sounds. A keyboard sat alongside the entirety of his collection, its bright white keys reflecting the distant blue moonlight that came though the window across the room. Everything was wired through countless connections into the large amp and speakers that sat beside his desk.

The music that was playing stopped, and Oliver awoke to what was going on, though he was too high to think much of it. He moved from his seat and onto a spot on the floor.

A low buzz came from the large speakers, and Mike began to quickly move about his desk. An echoing scale of ethereal notes played from his keyboard, looping into an ambient melody that sounded of harps falling through an endless crystalline cavern. Elegant noise erupted from the Game Boy in distorted waves, which slowly melded into droning chords that danced along with the falling harps. High-pitched glitches cut through the atmosphere, coming from the altered electronics that used to be his daughter's broken toys. The sound was at first intense, but it soon eased into soothing clatter that splattered the music with a subtle background noise, giving it a sincerity that could only arrive through the sound of imperfection.

The music traveled on, changing every once in awhile when Mike made it so. Eventually he stepped from his desk, satisfied with the ambient repetition that he had created.

"I was just everywhere," Oliver said, laughing from the floor.

"That's good, man," Mike replied, bouncing his head around with his eyes closed.

"Why the hell am I me?" Oliver asked.

"Because you can't be anyone else," Mike answered, sitting on the floor beside Oliver. "If you weren't you, you wouldn't be you. You'd be something else. And then you'd ask 'Why the hell am I me?' and it would be the same question but different."

"Just think of all the things that shape who we are. We're hardly ourselves, really. We're more like what's around us than what's within."

"Our childhood is what shapes us the most, which is a shame since it's when we have the least control over our lives."

"But maybe that's essential. Maybe if we had complete control over our creation we would be empty. We need that separate something within us to exist, no matter if it's good or bad. Without an external influence we'd be nothing."

"But the whole point of life is to lose that something. We have to see past what isn't our true nature."

"And see that we're empty?" Oliver asked, turning to Mike.

"Empty, but real."

"You don't even know what real is, man."

"Eh, you're right," Mike said, lying on the floor.

"When I think of what I want," Oliver said, "all that I can come up with is this fantastic existence. It's some grand adventure, the kind that doesn't happen in reality, where I just exist in some sort of heavenly place where I can do whatever I want. Nothing matters there, which makes it beautiful."

"Damn, man. So you want be a god?"

"I can't explain it."

"I understand. Everyone has their own view of paradise."

"When I was little I played this video game. It was my favorite for sure. You were this boy, this plain old white kid from some plain old town. All this crazy shit started to happen, but it was in this normal sort of world. Aliens and distorted realties and ghosts and shit. And this kid went on to be the hero. It was a trip for sure. Just imagine how it affected my little childhood mind. Why the hell do I want something amazing? Why do I want a life full of meaning and magic? Because I was raised in a fictional world where anything was possible and there was a point to everything! I lived and breathed a fiction that was poured into my head."

"Is that so bad?" Mike asked. "Maybe it opened up your mind. This world needs a little magic."

"Yeah, it is. Well, yeah and no. I dunno."

"What?"

"I mean it was good. It made me think differently, and it made me want to be more than what I am. All the stuff I was raised on, all the entertainment and fantasy, it was my reality. Yeah, I knew none of it was really real, but that didn't matter. It still shaped me and my desires. It changed how I thought about everything. And now look at me." Oliver sat up and turned to Mike. "I expect the fantastic from the unfantastic."

"I think life's pretty fantastic."

"Yeah, well, sometimes it is, I guess."

"Nice reply," Mike laughed.

"Think of all the shit that we were raised on, that kids nowadays are raised on. Hell, even think of all the shit adults are obsessed with. We live in a world of fantasy. We thrive for any escape from this cage of reality. We tell ourselves that we know the difference between entertainment and real life, but we don't see how surrounding ourselves with stories affects us. The way we think, what we judge as right and wrong, we learn from fucking fantasy! Our society is shaped by TV shows and movies and games and all kinds of other shit!"

"All the world's a stage," Mike added.

"It's all a story we tell ourselves. Reality is a void, and so we flood it with our own made up truths. Now we've confused those lies with what's real. We think our lives are the true nature of the universe, when really we're just a product of a society based upon fiction."

"How we communicate affects what we communicate. And what we communicate affects what we are."

"And how do we communicate? Entertainment. So now we're killing the planet and each other just because we want to have a good time."

"The question is, does it matter?"

"No, it probably doesn't," Oliver answered, lying back down. "If the truth is a lie to begin with, then our lies may as well be truths. Maybe I'm better off trying to escape into my fantasy. It might very well be as real as all of this."

"Remember," Mike said sitting up, "words don't mean a thing." He patted Oliver's shoulder and smiled. "When you think about life, you forget about it. So just exist, and you'll understand." He paused and seemed to think deeply. "Or at least you'll understand that there's nothing to understand."

"Yeah," Oliver said, lying still upon the floor. "I guess."

"That's all you can do," Mike smiled.

December 24th, 1981
Or, Elsewhere

Arthur was alone.

He hadn't gone home for the holidays. It was a long drive back to Moyenne, and he had too much to do anyway. His classes were over for the semester, so he gave most of his free time to working as a waiter at a local Chinese restaurant. It was run by two unbearable, middle-aged white men who treated him like shit. The work was long, monotonous, and infuriatingly dull. But he needed the money badly, even if it meant spending his days at such a place. His parents helped pay for his classes, but there was still a large portion of it he was responsible for, as well as all the money needed just to take care of himself and pay rent.

"No homemade pumpkin pie for me," he told his roommate as they were saying goodbye. "No happiness in a million ways."

"Well, just don't jerk off too much while you're sittin' around here all alone," his roommate said, patting him on the arm.

"Go to hell and have a merry Christmas," Arthur replied.

Four days had passed since then, four days that were spent either working or being in solitude. He was now sitting beside his living room window, reading *Zorba The Greek* and wishing he were more of a man. He wanted to be a fully alive human being, dancing with the beautiful world of which he was a part. He wanted to discover the truth of life within the very life that he lived, and not, as he was currently in a state of doing, within the cramped world inside his head.

Arthur set down his book and lit up a cigarette. He quickly snubbed it out after a few drags. He didn't really like smoking, but he could never seem to kick the habit of wanting one. So he let himself smoke when he needed, and usually stopped swiftly from the displeasure it gave him.

He gazed out of the window into the snow-covered street. There was a strong solitude at this time of year since it was a small college town. Most people were back home with their families.

The snow fell heavy and slow through the radiance of the streetlights outside his window. Arthur imagined himself out there, staring up into the sky, watching as the snowflakes fell past him like stars drifting through the universe.

He often daydreamed of not-so-distant things, beautiful visions of nearby heavens that were nothing more than average life. It was a way of making his mundane world a part of that which was truly remarkable. A sacred universe surrounded him, and within himself his mind could guide him anywhere across its beauty.

Arthur began to feel lonely. He hated to admit it. Most of the time he favored solitude. His thoughts could keep him company well enough, and he enjoyed the serenity he could discover only when he was alone, undistracted by the countless obligations that arose when he had to play the game of social interaction. But he was nevertheless still human, and a desire for companionship would nudge its way into his head. A single thought would be born with an insatiable urge to escape into another living being. The authenticity of its existence needed to be proven by that of another soul.

He stood and walked away from the winter scene of his window. Falling upon the living room sofa, he stared at the television without turning it on. He just gazed at a dark reflection bent upon the surface of the TV screen. His loneliness was quickly building as time passed by. Eventually his mind broke free and forced his body to take action. He threw on his winter coat, slid on his worn out boots, and left the warmth of his empty house.

Arthur wondered where he was heading. He had no goal in mind other than to interact with at least one person. He walked along the white sidewalks, heading towards the gas station a mile down the road. It was the only place he could imagine finding someone out at a time like this. It was a twenty-four hour place, and he knew he could at least share a few words with the attendant there.

Most of the houses he passed were vacantly dark. Every so often there would be one with Christmas lights strung across its windows and gutters, though only half of them were ever turned on. The rest hung like dead souls upon a string.

Arthur turned down the long road that led away from his small neighborhood. The gas station was at the far end of it, beside the highway that left town. The street that he was on was barren, though it at least had a wide, shoveled sidewalk he could follow. Dull orange streetlights illuminated his surroundings every hundred feet or so, and the cold trees to his right creaked in the wavering gusts of wind. The night sky was overcast and starless. The moon was mostly obscured, its glow vaguely dancing through thin gaps in the clouds.

Arthur's loneliness was frozen by the cold night air. It expanded and cracked the edges of his mind. His steps moved even faster in the hope that he would soon find someone to talk to.

He wondered why he felt so lonely. He had never felt such an urge to be with someone. Maybe it was the holidays? Maybe he missed the days he used to spend with his family at this time of the year?

Or maybe it was something more?

Was he yearning for a deeper bond?

A love that could walk with him through life?

He remembered the last relationship he was in. In his senior year of high school he dated Kelly Russell for eight months. He even began to think he loved her, but then she left him for reasons he never knew. One day in June she told him they couldn't be together, though she wouldn't say why. She merely kissed him on the cheek and said goodbye. After that he hadn't been in a steady relationship, and the only intimacy he found was in the few drunken affairs he stumbled upon after parties, which in truth he could hardly call intimate at all.

Arthur stopped beside an empty park. He stared at its desolate, snow-covered playground and imagined it in the warmth of summer when it was filled with life. In a quick decision he walked his way across the small field of white and stood beside a lonely swing set. With a single motion he swept away the snow upon its seat and sat down. He pushed himself forward and back a few times before his ass felt too cold and he jumped up and left. He continued on towards the gas station as if he had never stopped.

He saw a glow of lights behind trees in the distance. His pace quickened as the glow grew larger. He eventually found himself in front of the gas station that he sought so dearly. He pulled at the front door and felt the warmth of its interior greet him.

"Hi," he said, smiling at the attendant, who was an older man with a long, graying, red beard and sad-looking eyes. His lips were rather large, and they glistened in the bright fluorescent lights of the gas station.

"Hi," the attendant said back, glancing at Arthur and then turning his eyes back down at the magazine in his hands.

Arthur wasn't sure what else to do. He didn't really need anything besides someone to talk to, so he wandered around the store looking for anything at all to buy. He gave up and decided to just get a pack of cigarettes even though he didn't need them.

"Camel Lights, please," Arthur said, walking up to the cashier. The man turned and grabbed a pack from the wall behind him in a clearly routine motion.

"Seventy-nine cents," he said, setting the pack down.

Arthur pulled out his wallet and gave the man a dollar.

"Some weather out there," he said in hopes of getting a few more words out of the man.

"Yeah, it's winter," is all he replied.

They stood silent as the man counted out Arthur's change.

"Thanks," Arthur said as he was handed two dimes and a penny.

"Yup," the attendant mumbled, looking back down at his magazine, which Arthur quickly glanced at, half expecting it to be a porno mag, though it wasn't. The man was reading an old crinkled up issue of *Sports Review Wrestling*. On its cover were men with ruined faces covered in blood, along with a small picture in the corner of two bikini-clad women fighting.

"Bye," Arthur said, walking backwards to the door.

"Bye," the man replied, not looking up.

As Arthur began to turn towards the door he felt a quick rush of cold wind come inward into the warm store. Before him stood a face he somehow knew, though it took him a moment to really recognize.

"Lisa?" he asked, hoping he was right.

"Arthur?" she replied with a confused smile on her face.

He hadn't seen her in years, not since she moved away his freshman year of high school.

"What are you doing here?" he asked and then quickly corrected himself. "I mean, hello and how are you? But also, what are you doing here?"

"I'm good. I'm good," she said, nodding and brushing her blonde hair aside. "I go to school here. And you?"

"Me too," he answered, fiddling with the pack of Camels in his hand.

"Wow, really?" she said, rubbing her hands against her arms.

"Oh, jeeze," Arthur said, quickly stepping back. "I'll get outta your way so you can warm up."

"I never knew you went here," Lisa said, walking closer.

"Me neither. I mean I never knew you did too. I knew I did."

"Yeah," she laughed.

"Yeah," he said, smiling back as his loneliness melted away.

This Will Be A Memory
Or, Ochre

Faye watched her grandma stir as if it were magic. She was mesmerized by the skill and ease with which she mixed the cookie dough. Her arm would pull upwards and spin about before rushing back down and, with a twist of the wrist, begin the short cycle again.

"Don't you love chocolate chips?" her grandma asked.

"Yeah," Faye uttered, still staring at her grandma, who had walked away to get a spoon from a nearby drawer.

"Let's put them on the tray," her grandma said, looking to her. Faye smiled and nodded yes, jumping down from the small stool she stood on and walking to the kitchen table. She sat with her knees bent beneath her upon the yellow-green kitchen chair. She reached for the cookie sheet, sliding it closer to her.

"I'll hand you a spoonful," her grandma said, "and you plop it down. Okay?"

"Okay," Faye answered, worriedly excited.

Her grandma took the spoon and dipped it into the bowl of dough, passing it to Faye afterwards. It felt heavy in her small hand, and she imagined the rather large cookie it would soon turn into.

She held the spoon over the cookie tray and shook it quickly down, slopping the dough into an oblong mess.

"No, no," her grandma spoke gently, though shaking her head. "Like this." She took the spoon from Faye and grabbed another dollop of cookie dough. She held it over the baking sheet and with her thumb slid it away from the spoon. It landed with a tender thud upon the tray. She gathered another spoonful of dough and handed it to Faye. "Careful now."

"Mmhm," Faye mumbled, grabbing the spoon. She held it above the tray, pausing for a moment to think about what to do next. She suddenly moved her other hand over and pressed her thumb into the dough. It sunk into the mixture. Faye had to use her other fingers to get it away from the spoon and her skin. Finally, it fell beside her previous disaster on the cookie sheet.

"Good job," her grandma said, patting her on the back. "We've got lots more to do." Faye smiled and waited for another spoonful. After placing six or seven of them down onto the tray, she began to feel a bit bored. She had mastered the art of cookie dough, and her thoughts were ready for more exciting things to do.

She wondered what her classmates were up to. All of the elementary school students had the day off for some sort of teacher workday. Earlier in the morning Faye had gotten to lie around in her pajamas, laughing at Claire for having to go to school. Afterwards her father took her to spend the day at her grandparents'. She was excited because she enjoyed the strange things they did, like feeding ducks and doing jigsaw puzzles.

"Why don't you take a break and go sit with your grandpa," her grandma said, sensing Faye's boredom. "I'll finish up the cookies. And in a little while I'm sure I'll need help eating them."

"Okay," Faye answered, stepping down from her chair. She meandered across the house to the living room, where her grandpa sat watching television. His eyes gleamed and a smile broke across his face as he saw Faye walk into the room.

"Well, hello," his rough voice spoke.

"Hello," she answered, sitting on the brown velvet sofa beside his chair. She turned to the television, where she saw a man painting with what looked like a flat piece of metal. He brushed on streaks of white across a patch of grayish blue, and instantly Faye recognized a small pond of water against a green shore.

"Do you like painting?" her grandpa asked.

"Yeah," she answered, keeping her eyes upon the television.

"So does your brother," he continued. "He likes it quite a lot. Maybe someday you could be a painter too." She shrugged her shoulders in response. She was too mesmerized by the man on the television to really answer. His hair was stranger than any she had seen before. It was large and round and seemed soft like foam. His voice was low and calm like her grandpa's, though less rough than his. He happily spoke of the trees, lakes, and mountains that he painted on the canvas beside him.

Faye sat watching the show until the man was finished with his picture. As the credits began to roll, her eyes drifted from the television to the rest of the room. The sunlight was shining in through the cream colored curtains behind her, and the warm yellow walls were glowing with comfort in Faye's mind. She turned to her grandpa and found that he was watching her.

"What?" she laughed, startled to find that she was being watched, though happy it was by her grandpa.

"What?" he asked back, shrugging his shoulders.

"Why are you watching me?" she demanded.

"How do you know I was watching you?"

"I saw you!"

"If you saw me watching you then you had to be watching me! How else would you know?"

She thought about it and couldn't answer, so instead she tumbled to her side and fell into the crevice of the couch. She breathed in the dusty smell of old velvet. For some reason the scent awoke powerful thoughts of death, the very same ones that had recently invaded her life. No real notions came to her head, but she felt the strange sensation that would arise when she knew she thinking about dying. It felt heavy all over her body, yet at the same time made her feel like nothing at all.

"Hello?" her grandpa said after a while.

She didn't move.

"Hello? Hello?" he repeated.

She pulled herself up and looked to the television in a sort of instinctual reaction to numb her feelings, but nothing comfortable was there. A man was shaving away at a wooden board with a strange tool Faye didn't recognize.

"So, how would you like to go to the museum today?" her grandpa asked.

She only half heard him. Her thoughts were stuck in between the image of the man woodworking on television and her innocent contemplations of mortality.

"Faye," he spoke a little louder, which pulled her attention away. She turned to him. "What're you thinking about?" he asked.

"Dying," she said inadvertently, immediately regretting so.

"Why are you thinking about that?" he asked.

"Because," she replied.

"Because why?" he pressed on with an expression that Faye couldn't understand. He seemed both happy and sad at the same time.

"Because someday I'll die. Someday everyone dies," she answered, staring into a vacant spot upon the warm yellow wall across the room.

Her grandpa stood from his seat and slowly moved nearer. He sat beside her on the sofa and patted his hand upon her leg.

"You're right," he told her. "Everyone does die someday. But that only makes life more special. Imagine if everyone lived forever. The world would be a mess! It would be too crowded! We all have our turn here, and then we move on so that the next people can live in our place. But what made you think about dying, dear? You don't have to worry about that for a long, long time."

"I dunno," she said, hiding her reasons in the hope that she could change the subject. "Don't tell anyone."

"And why not?" he asked.

"Because," she answered.

"Because why?" he continued, though this time she recognized his teasing expression. She didn't have a reason why, other than that she was embarrassed by it, which she knew wouldn't be a good enough reason to say. So she kept quiet and turned to the television, watching as the man upon the screen cut away at what looked like the wooden leg of a table.

"I won't tell anyone if you make me a promise," her grandpa said.

She looked back to him.

"What?" she asked.

"You have to promise me you won't get so sad about it. Dying may seem scary, but it's just a part of life. And you also have to promise me that if you get scared thinking about it that you'll talk to someone. Okay?"

She nodded yes and turned back to the TV, pushing the situation away. Her grandpa hugged her lightly.

"So, as I was saying, do you want to go to the museum today?" he asked.

"Yeah," she said with a smile.

"Good," he replied. "We can learn about all sorts of dead people there." This made her face cringe, and he gently laughed to ease her discomfort.

"I shouldn't have said that," he spoke to himself, shaking his head and grinning. "How about we take some cookies with us?"

Her sad face turned into a smile as her childhood came rushing back in. She had forgotten about the cookies she and her grandma had made. By now they were probably done.

The man on TV began to laugh, and for a moment Faye felt as if it was at her. But as she turned to the television she saw that he had accidentally cut his finger.

"Well, that's life," he said, bleeding small drops of red onto the wooden shavings at his feet.

Somebody Else Within You
Or, After All Your Good-Byes

Of all the things that reminded Claire of her mother, the color orange made her the saddest. It wasn't that every shade affected her. Only a certain hue in a certain light pulled at her heartstrings.

It was because Claire's mother wore a shirt of that particular color on the last day they saw each other. It wrapped in gentle folds around her body, and Claire, hugging her tight, shoved her face into that soft sea of tangerine-colored cotton.

She missed her mother badly as she cut a sweet potato into imperfect little cubes. Its warm shades blended with the cold lights of the kitchen, and the color that erupted from it was the exact one in which her mother left her life. Claire pushed her knife through its tough flesh, and with each slice she felt her sadness grow. She had learned not to stop it. That would only make it build up inside of her, releasing in a flood of sorrow later on. Instead she let it slowly rain onto her thoughts, where she would drift upon the pools of memory and sadness that arose within her.

"Please tell me there's butter in here," Jeanne said, opening the refrigerator.

"Behind the milk," Claire said.

"Good," Jeanne replied, grabbing the half-used stick of butter. "Can't have sweet potatoes without butter."

"Yeah," Claire agreed, finishing up her chopping and dumping the cubed sweet potatoes into a frying pan. She walked to the kitchen table and let Jeanne take over the cooking. Rubbing her fingers into her eyes as she sat down, she thought about her mother and what she would have cooked for the family tonight if she were still alive.

"Your dad and Faye should be here soon," Jeanne said as she stirred a chunk of melting butter into the pan of sizzling sweet potatoes. "Your grandparents are coming too."

Claire decided her mom would bake a thick loaf of bread that would fill the entire house with its wonderful smell. And she would cook a big pot of black bean soup with hints of spices that warmed whoever ate it and made them forget about the cold outside.

She watched Jeanne's movements as she cooked, comparing her to her mother and quickly deciding that she would rather have the woman she missed than the woman who stood in front of her. Instantly Claire regretted thinking so. She didn't mean to judge Jeanne. She just longed for the mother that was taken from her so long ago.

"Dinner should be nice," Claire said, standing up and moving beside her father's girlfriend. She half smiled as their eyes met, and Jeanne returned it with a full one.

"Your father's wanted this for a while," she replied, "and he just couldn't wait until Christmas."

The sound of the front door opening and closing reached the kitchen, and Claire waited for someone familiar to walk into the room.

"Hello," her brother spoke from the living room.

Claire moved to the doorway and leaned into the living room. She waved at Oliver as she held onto the wall with one hand.

"Hello," he said again, sitting heavily down on the couch. "Where is everyone?"

"Dad should be home soon," Claire answered. "Grandma and Grandpa and Faye should be here any minute too."

"M'kay," Oliver mumbled, staring blankly at the window across the room. Claire gave a small sigh and walked back to the kitchen. Jeanne was busy cooking, so she went into the dining room to be alone. She sat down upon one of the thin wooden chairs beside the table. Its legs creaked from old age as her weight shifted against it.

"Hello!" her father yelled out as he came in through the front door.

Claire heard the footsteps of others quickly follow his voice.

She didn't want to face her family yet. She was too adrift in her sadness. They would see right through her and know what she was thinking. She wasn't ashamed of her grief. It was more that she didn't want to weigh down her family with their cares for her happiness. She wanted their night together to be a good one.

She forced a smile, damming up the melancholy that her memories had stirred. Her family was home, including her mother, who sat deeply in her thoughts. The sadness would have to wait, rising higher and higher inside of her. She would have to face it later as it poured out from her eyes.

The Universe Is Warm With Light
Or, The Love Of Those Around You

"You smell like cigarettes," Oliver's grandmother said as she gave him a hug. He doubted on the way over whether or not he should have one, and now he regretted giving in to his craving.

"Sorry," he said as they stepped apart. "It was only one. I don't do it that much."

"Funny," she replied, "that's what your grandpa says too."

"It's a family curse," Oliver's father cut in. "One that I was able to leave behind, and I'm sure Oliver will too." He gave a dry smile as he looked to his son. He then turned to his father with the same expression. "Though I think Dad's just too far gone."

"Too far gone?" the old man replied. "I can shake anything. I'm my own master." He turned to his wife, who was giving him a look of contempt. "It just so happens that I enjoy tobacco, and dammit, I'll be dead someday anyway."

"Well, we all know that," she answered him. "I just don't want you smelling of it anymore. I'm tired of that awful scent clinging to everything you touch."

Oliver managed to slide away from the conversation, as he often did. He walked his way into the kitchen where he found Jeanne finishing up dinner. She glanced at him and smiled.

"Hello, Oliver," she said, turning back to her work. "How was your day?"

"Good," he answered. It was how he always replied to the question, even if it wasn't true. "How about you?"

"Beautiful," she replied. "I love a good winter day. The cold may be harsh, but it brings us closer together." She turned off the stove and waved the spoon in her hand. "Done!"

She began to bustle around the kitchen, straightening the odds and ends that were strewn about, so Oliver wandered his way into the dining room where he met Claire sitting alone. Her eyes gave away a recent sadness that was still there yet buried deep inside. It faintly echoed from her mind, and Oliver could sense its vague resonance.

"You okay?" he asked, sitting in the empty chair beside her.

"Yeah," she said, twisting in her seat. "You?"

"I'm good," he replied. "So what's wrong?"

"Nothing, really."

"If you say so."

She looked down at her feet and then quickly back up to him.

"I was—," she choked, her voice getting caught in her throat. She paused briefly and then continued. "I was thinking about Mom. Just missing her, ya know?"

"Yeah, I know," he said, looking his sister in the eyes, which was something he didn't often do to anyone at all. "I miss her too, even after all these years."

"It's not a sharp sadness, or at least right now it isn't," she said. "It's like a dull ache."

"That's what time does," he told her, sinking down deeper into a slouch. "It irons out your pains and makes them flat. They'll always be there, just not so sharply. They get smooth and stretched out all across your soul, or whatever it is, until you don't even really feel them anymore. But really they've become your skin, and they change who you are without you even noticing it."

"You've got quite a way with words, Oliver," she said.

"Eh, too bad they don't really mean anything," he replied with a smile. "If they did I might actually figure this thing out."

"What thing?" she asked.

"Life, ya know?"

"Yeah, I know," she said, rolling her eyes.

"Could you give me a hand, Claire?" Jeanne asked, walking into the room with a large dish of some sort of casserole. She placed it upon the center of the table.

"Sure," Claire answered, standing up.

"Can I do anything?" Oliver asked.

"Why don't you find Faye," Jeanne told him, "and make sure she washes her hands."

"Mhmm," he replied, standing from his chair. He walked to the living room, where his father and grandparents were talking about some relative or other.

"Where's Faye?" he asked them, standing with his hands buried deep in the pockets of his jeans.

"She's upstairs," his father answered. "She's in a mood. Why don't you try talking to her?"

"I suppose," Oliver replied.

"She's seven years old and worried about dying," Oliver's grandfather said, shaking his head. "Though you didn't hear it from me. I promised I wouldn't tell. I wish I could see those little thoughts of hers. What does a seven-year-old think about death?"

"Lots," Oliver said. "When I was that little I was afraid of everything, especially dying. I thought about it a lot. Every kid does once they realize they're alive."

"Maybe she needs someone like you, her brother," his father told him. Oliver doubtfully nodded yes, though he really did hope he could help her. He cared for his little sister, and he could remember how strange it was to be her age. Everything around had the ability to either be completely wonderful or utterly terrifying. The realization that you and everyone you knew would someday die was a heavy point in childhood. What his sister was thinking now would be important in shaping who she would become.

He made his way up the stairway and down the hallway to Faye's room. Her door was half open, and Oliver could hear the sound of her small radio playing music from within.

He leaned into the doorway and knocked upon the wall.

"Hi, Faye," he said.

"Hi," she answered, sitting on her bed and looking through a large children's book.

"What're you reading?" he asked, moving closer.

"A book," she answered mockingly, though without any real resentment towards him. She was simply an angry seven-year-old, and he could tell that she was mad at the entire world, which he just so happened to be a part of.

"What's it about?" he asked, sitting beside her.

"Nothing," she replied, shutting the book and turning to him. "Me and grandpa went to the museum today."

"Oh yeah?" he asked. "How was it?"

"Did you know about world war?" she asked back.

"Yup," he said, nodding his head.

"There were two of them," she told him.

"And they were pretty bad," he added. "Lots of people got hurt."

"You think there'll be a third?" she asked, fidgeting about.

"No, I don't," he answered, though he actually did believe there would be.

"And we saw cavemen," she said, suddenly seeming to drift into other thoughts, "and statues of weird things, and old cars."

"Sounds pretty cool," he told her.

"Yeah," she said, scooting off of the bed and walking to her small, pink stereo. She turned the quiet pop music off and faced Oliver. "Is dinner done?"

"Uhm, yes," he answered. "Listen, are you okay?"

"Yup," she replied, walking towards the door and then out of the room. "C'mon!" she yelled from the hallway.

Arthur bit his lower lip and nodded to himself. He sat upon Faye's small, pink bed and looked around her room, imagining the strange childhood world she lived in. He thought of the bizarre existence that children faced, a world entirely mysterious to them, yet at the same time a world that they must grow into without a choice.

Faye ran back to her room and stood in the doorway.

"C'mon!" she yelled again.

"I'm coming," Oliver groaned, standing up from the low-lying bed. He walked to her and patted her head, to which she nudged him away and smiled.

"You know I hate that, Ollie," she said.

"And you know I hate being called Ollie," he replied, walking beside her down the hallway. "It sounds like a name for a dog."

"Ollie! Ollie! Ollie!" she yelled, running down the steps.

Oliver followed close behind, though at a much slower pace. When Faye reached the bottom she turned to run into the kitchen. Jeanne quickly yelled at her for doing so, and Oliver could hear Faye's laughter as she ran out of the kitchen and into the dining room.

"I see you did something good," Oliver's father said, smiling.

"I guess so," Oliver replied. "I didn't really do much."

"Let's hope she stays in a good mood," his grandmother said, slowly standing from her chair. The four of them walked to the dining room, where Faye and Claire sat talking.

"Faye, wash your hands," her father told her, walking past the table and into the kitchen to help Jeanne. Faye shot up and ran to the bathroom to do so, while everyone else took their place at the table. An awkward silence arose as Oliver and Claire sat alone with their grandparents.

"So, when is your last day?" Claire's grandmother asked her, finally breaking the quiet.

"This Friday," she answered. "I'm really excited."

"I bet you are," her grandmother said, nodding and seeming to think deeply about it. The awkward silence returned, though this time it was cut short by Faye's return.

"Do you think we'll be in a museum someday?" Faye asked, sitting beside her grandpa.

"Well, sure," he answered. "You kids will be at least. You'll all do amazing things. And someday they'll say 'Those Radcliffs were something else!'"

"Oliver will be in an art museum for his paintings," Faye said, leaning onto the table and playing with her silverware. "I'll be in a history museum for being the first girl president. And Claire will be in a science museum."

"A science museum?" Claire asked from across the table.

"Yup," Faye replied, "you'll be there for being the funniest looking big sister."

"Oh, good one," Claire said.

"That's not nice," Faye's grandma told her, though Faye seemed to not hear as she squirmed around in her chair.

Oliver was thinking about his paintings and whether or not they really would be in a museum someday. He laughed at himself for being so lost in thought over a comment made by his little sister, but it nonetheless stirred his self-doubt. He wondered if another human being would ever appreciate his work.

"Lets eat!" Jeanne proclaimed as she and Arthur walked into the room carrying the final trays of food. She set a large dish of steaming sweet potato pilaf down in front of Oliver's grandfather.

"Everything looks great, Jeanne," he told her, setting his hand on her back as she leaned past him.

"Let's hope it tastes good too," she replied with a smile.

Oliver tried to pull himself out of his head so he could be with his family, but his self-absorbed feelings where heavy. After some time he was finally able to leave them behind, though he fell into another heap of thoughts that took him in a different direction.

He thought about the people that now sat around him. He felt happy being with them, his family, but at the same time he felt that he wasn't himself. It was as if he put up some sort of theatric portrayal of the best parts of his personality.

If he wasn't himself, who was he then?

And who where these people to him if he wasn't Oliver?

He got fed up with his brain's chatter and forced his thoughts to go quiet. He simply sat at his chair and ate the food in front of him, listening to the conversation of his family. They talked about work and the weather and school and the food that they ate. At one point the conversation nearly drifted into the topic of the recent tragedy on the subway, but Oliver's father quickly changed the subject before Faye could realize it.

Oliver began to feel bored, and then began to feel bad for being bored. He was happy to be with his family, but at the same time he wondered if being happy went hand in hand with being bored.

He chewed on a spoonful of peas, crushing them slowly between his teeth, while he thought about being somewhere else. The muscles in his body worked together, pulling the food down his throat and into his stomach, where it met a complex mixture of chemicals that would convert it into energy and waste. The energy would be used to fuel Oliver's body and mind. The waste would be shat out hours later into a toilet.

Oliver imagined himself on the coast somewhere, walking in the water with some beautiful woman and talking about beautiful things. She touched him, and he touched her.

The mushed peas in his stomach were being pulled apart by enzymes and acid. The sweet potatoes he had swallowed a little earlier were already moving into his small intestines, where they would be stripped of everything his body needed.

Oliver pictured himself alone atop a tall building as the sun was setting across an abandoned city landscape. He jumped off the edge of the rooftop and gently drifted down, watching as the windows full of colored light slowly flew past him. He stopped before touching the ground and floated back up in reverse.

"Oliver?" his father asked.

"Huh?" he replied.

"Sometimes I wonder where you go," he said, "but then I remember you're my son and that you're just lost somewhere inside that head of yours."

To this Oliver smiled. He was shoved back into reality, and he remembered being happily bored with his family.

"How's your painting going?" his grandpa asked. "Still making colorful splatters?"

"Yes, I am," Oliver answered, well used to the question. "It's going fine. I just finished one I really like a few days ago."

"Are you going to show anyone?" his grandma asked, leaning over her plate and looking to him.

"I'd like to," he replied, scooping up a forkful of food and holding it in front of him, hoping to change the subject with his apparent desire to eat.

"That's good," she said, leaning back into her chair.

"Yeah," Oliver mumbled before shoving the casserole into his mouth. His brain told his body exactly what to do with the food inside of him as he again drifted away into a dream of somewhere else.

December 24th, 1985
Or, First Comes Love

Her tongue slid softly against his before hiding behind her lips. His hand rested against her neck, slowly wandering across her skin. He opened his eyes and smiled. She did the same.

"I love you," he told her.

"I love you too," she whispered back.

"Now," he said loudly, breaking the moment apart into another mood, "just smile at my dad and be polite with my mom, and everything will go fine. He's a sucker for cute girls like you, and if my mom thinks you're well-mannered then you'll be more than good enough for me."

"I am well-mannered," she said, folding her arms and giving him an eye. "Don't you think so?"

"No, I don't," he teased, pulling her back in for one more kiss.

They got out of Arthur's red Chevette and walked to the shoveled sidewalk of his parents' house. Bright walls of snow nearly half a foot high lined the dark wet sidewalk. Arthur could tell his father had just shoveled this morning.

They walked up the three steps that led to the patio, and Arthur knocked a few times on the front door. He felt strange doing so. Most of his life he had just walked right it. But this wasn't his home anymore. He had to knock.

The door made clunking sounds as someone on the other side unlocked it. Arthur pulled Mia close just as the door swung open. His mother stood smiling, wearing a long, glossy jade skirt and a dark emerald and red plaid blouse.

"So you must be Mia?" she asked.

"Yes, ma'am," Mia replied, smiling and quickly glancing at Arthur. He stepped into the doorway and gave his mom a hug.

"Missed you," he said, squeezing her tight.

"I missed you too," she told him, "so much."

As he moved away from his mother his hand floated back to grab Mia's. He pulled her in through the doorway, and they stood in the brightly lit living room of his parents' house. His mother had opened wide the front window curtains, and the crisp blue winter sky was shining in. Arthur stood in the familiar space and smelled his mother's cooking, breathing in a heavy lungful of air to enjoy it.

"It smells wonderful in here," Mia said, letting go of Arthur and placing her hands in her pockets.

"Thank you," Arthur's mother replied, tilting her head. "I'm glad to have someone else here besides Frank to enjoy my cooking." Her tone turned into a near whisper. "All that man ever wants is junk food." Arthur gave a small laugh and looked to Mia.

"Well, I'm sure we'll enjoy it quite a bit," he said, turning back to his mother. "You did make it vegetarian, didn't you?"

"Oh, yes," she said with a half-smile. "Though it wasn't easy." She looked to Mia, who had an uncomfortable expression on her face. "I do hope you like it."

"I can tell I will from the smell alone," Mia replied, the nervous look on her face easing.

"Frank insisted we at least have some ham," Arthur's mother continued, "so there is that."

"Where is Dad?" Arthur asked, taking off his coat and then helping Mia with hers.

"Right here," his father said, walking into the room and chewing on a piece of ham that he snuck away from the kitchen.

"Would you wait five minutes, dear," Arthur's mother sighed.

"Sorry, Rose," he said to his wife, "but I'm hungry." He turned to Mia and smiled. She wore a lightly colored, loose argyle sweater and tight black pants. Her dark hair was held back in a ponytail, and her long bangs fell across the sides of her face. Wide hooped earrings dangled from her ears and glistened gold in the sunlight that came through the windows.

She smiled back at Arthur's father.

"Ah, is this Lisa?" he asked.

Arthur coughed and fidgeted his hands together.

"Mia, Dad," he quickly said. "This is Mia."

"Oh dear," his father laughed, rubbing one of his hands against his thinning head of hair.

"So, who is this Lisa?" Mia asked, turning to Arthur and giving him a playfully glare. She already knew of Lisa and wanted nothing other than to make the situation more amusing.

Arthur had met Mia only a month after breaking up with Lisa, who had dumped him because, according to her, they had nothing in common. It was true, and Arthur accepted it, but he nonetheless was solidly depressed for a month. His sadness only left because he met a woman who was even more beautiful, inside and out.

Arthur had gotten a job writing for the small literary magazine *The Sparrow Tree,* and during his second week he was assigned an interview with a local writer named Mia Simon. He fell in love with her before they even met. He read her short story about a homeless man who spoke to trees, and her every word seduced him into a romantic dream. Her prose spoke to him more deeply than anyone else's words ever had, and the meaning within her writing expressed, Arthur believed, what it meant to be fully human, fully alive.

He had a small black and white photo of her that the magazine had given him along with her story, and he spent much of his time gazing at it, imagining the moment when they would meet. The day before their interview he forced himself to calm down and be rational. He didn't want to become infatuated with someone he didn't even know, and he definitely didn't want to come off as strange and obsessive. This worked at first, and up until he met her he was calm and collected, but as soon as he saw her sitting alone at the café where they were to meet, sipping coffee and staring out of the window at the people that walked by, he was a love-struck mess.

It wasn't long before Mia felt something for him as well. Perhaps it was his awkward sincerity, which spilled out through his mumbled words. Maybe it was the way he understood her writing, talking about it as if he knew her thoughts, as if he completely understood her, which no one else had ever done. Or perhaps it was simply his looks. His light blue eyes that seemed to gaze deeply into every inch of the world around him. His dark, short beard that grew from his rugged face. His well-kept, yet long, hair. His strong-looking hands, which shuffled with a nervous manner against the table between them, betraying his interest in her.

With the speed at which they connected it was most likely all of these things. Before the night was finished, after walking her home through the cool October twilight, Arthur would leave with her telephone number. On their first date, which was a matter of fact they settled during Arthur's nervous phone call, they kissed beside the glowing amber lights of a fall festival parade. Their lips made love as shimmering jack-o-lanterns danced past and the cool autumn breeze brought their bodies closer together.

Over the next few weeks they grew into each other's lives, realizing more every day that they were made for one another. Often times they would do nothing at all besides lie together and talk until the morning light broke into one of their apartments. Mia would speak to him in French, which she had learned in childhood from her grandparents, and which Arthur didn't understand at all. Arthur would ramble on about the books he had read and the ideas that needed to pour out of his mind.

The months quickly passed, and the two of them became inseparable. A year after they had met, Arthur asked her if she would like to move in with him. She did, and they made their small home together in his fifth-story apartment.

As they lazed about together one Sunday evening in late November, Arthur looked to her with a smile.

"Come with me to Moyenne," he said, "and meet my family."

"Oui, mon amour," she replied, tossing her notebook full of jotted down stories aside and climbing on top of him. Within a month she would be standing in his parent's living room, waiting for Arthur's reply to the embarrassing situation his father created.

"She's no one," he said, grinning. "No one at all."

"That's right," Mia said back.

"I like her," Arthur's father chuckled. "She's gonna put this boy in his place."

"His place," Arthur's mother said, "and yours, is at the table. The food is almost done." She turned to Mia, who was standing nearly silhouetted before the bright windows. "Mia, could you help me finish up?"

"Sure," Mia replied with a slight hesitation. She looked to Arthur. He wore a large grin on his face, and she in turn gave him the faintest scowl. His mother walked into the kitchen, and Mia followed.

Arthur and his father moved to the dining room, where they sat at the neatly set table.

"She seems like a nice girl," his father said, shifting in his seat and impatiently looking around. He was clearly tired of waiting for the food to be done, specifically the ham that had been cooling for some time now.

"She is," Arthur replied.

The two sat quietly listening to the distant noise in the kitchen. Arthur could make out Mia's faint voice, along with his mother's, and he wondered what it was they were talking about.

"Don't worry," his father said, "your mom will be kind to her. She's just glad to see you getting serious with someone. She wants grandkids bad, you know?"

"Well, that's not gonna happen for a long time," Arthur said, shaking his head. "Hell, we're not even married."

"Yeah, we'll see," his father replied, again looking anxious for the food. "How's work going?"

"Good. I'm writing regularly now, articles and such. And I'm getting ready to start a book."

"That's good to hear. As long as you're getting paid well. You are getting paid, right?"

"Yes, I'm getting paid, Dad."

"I know you are. I'm just being your father. What does Mia do for a living?"

"She writes too, but for now she's working at a movie theater just to make some money."

"Oh, well, movies are good. Old ones at least. None of that *Back To The Future* stuff. Does she like *Back To The Future*?"

"Actually, no, she doesn't."

"Good."

"So how are you and Mom?"

"We're good. We're good," his father replied. "Not much going on around here." He stood from his seat and began to meander out of the room. "I'm gonna have a smoke."

"Okay," Arthur replied. He watched his father walk out of the room and then shortly later walk by the doorway with his coat on and a cigarette in hand. Mia entered the dining room with a smile on her face.

"Hello," Arthur said to her as she sat down beside him.

"Hello," she replied, resting her hand upon his, "and Merry Christmas." She gave him a quick kiss just before his mother walked in.

"Don't tell me Frank is out there smoking, for God's sake," she said, setting the cooked ham upon the table. The smell of it filled the room, and Arthur could tell it made Mia feel sick. It slightly did the same to him too, since he hadn't eaten meat in nearly half a year.

His mother quickly left in search of her smoking husband, leaving Arthur and Mia alone again. They looked at each other and nodded at nothing in particular.

"Merry Christmas," Arthur said, turning to stare at the cooked ham.

The End Of You
Or, What Will Most Certainly Happen

Faye sat alone in her bedroom with the door nearly shut all the way. She could hear her dad and sister downstairs watching some movie about something she didn't care about. She told them she didn't want to watch it and that she wanted to play in her room. It was true that she didn't want to see it, but it had been a small lie when she said she wanted to play. She was instead sitting on the floor beside her bed, reading her book on death.

Faye was looking over the index of chapters in *Transience Within: Our Views On Death*, trying to figure out where to begin. She had only read one book with chapters before, and it was nothing compared to what she held in her hands. It was just a kid's book about magic and such with only four or five chapters at most. What she was reading now had lots of chapters with names she didn't understand and hundreds of pages of little printed words.

She decided to start at the beginning, which was "Chapter One: Life." She took a deep breath and read slowly out loud. Her voice hesitated at every word she didn't understand, which happened often.

To write a book about death, one must first define what death is. To define death, one must first define life. There is no dying without living. (Yet could there be living without dying?)
Life is the existence of a dynamic being.
Living is the subsistence of that being.
Life and living are energy.
Death is the inexistence of a dynamic being.
Dying is the cessation of that being.
Death and dying are emptiness.

Faye stopped at this point to think about what she was doing. It took her nearly ten minutes just to get through those few sentences, though she did get through them nonetheless. Many of the words she couldn't understand, even if she was able to sound them out. What she did comprehend she tried to sum up in her head.

Death was the end of life.

Life was being alive.

Death was the end of being alive.

This led her to an even greater problem.

What would it feel like to not be alive?

Faye began to sense fear creep into her thoughts. She didn't want to die. She didn't want to not exist. She wasn't even sure what that would be like, since she had always existed.

Then, for a brief moment of clarity, especially for a child her age, she thought about her father. He was alive before she was, which meant she didn't always exist. Did that mean she had been dead before?

Her innocent fear began to slowly fade into curiosity, though a stain of childish terror still lingered in her thoughts. She wanted to know the answers to her questions, but she was afraid of what she might find. She decided to continue with her book, leaving behind what she had just read and flipping the pages forward until an image caught her eye. It was a large wheel held by an eerie, though also a little silly, red-faced monster. In the wheel were all sorts of little drawings split up into sections. Some of them were happy scenes, where people were talking and working and playing music together. And there were special-looking people floating around on clouds and sitting about in dazzling colors. But on the bottom half were people and animals that didn't seem so happy. They were fighting and running and, as far as Faye could tell, dying in very bad ways.

She looked to the page beside the image, where the title of the chapter sat in large italic letters.

Chapter Seven: The View Of Reincarnation

Faye wondered what the word reincarnation meant, along with how she was supposed to pronounce it. She started to read in hopes of finding out.

Reincarnation, the idea of continuation after death into another life (which consequently brings the belief in lives previous to the current), is a view that has long been a part of human thought. Often it is connected with

Buddhism and other Eastern religions, though it has played an important part in the Western view of life and death as well.

Karma, or the cycle of cause and effect brought about by one's actions and deeds, is the spinning of the wheel of life and death. It leads a soul (a term which may or may not fit, depending on the doctrine of belief, though it is used here merely for its ease of use) through its countless lives, and the soul in turn is the one that creates the karma. An endless cycle is formed, which many doctrines say can be escaped through self-discipline and wisdom.

Faye stopped again after reading for quite some time. She thought about what she had just taken in. Of the words she understood she formed a simple idea of rebirth in her mind. The image of the wheel helped fuel her imagination, and a strange new awareness came to her head.

She had lived before as other people or animals, and would live again after she died. All she had to do was be good, and she wouldn't really have anything to worry about. This notion actually calmed her, since the idea of nothingness after death was, to her, terrifying. To be absolutely nothing at all, she thought, was the worst thing to be.

She wasn't afraid of going to someplace bad. That would never happen, since she believed herself to be a good person. And she wasn't afraid of the difficulties she would face, since good would always prevail. It was nothingness that she feared, and reincarnation was the hopeful answer to that.

Faye had grown tired of reading her difficult book. She couldn't imagine being able to read the whole thing, so she began to shut it by quickly flipping through the pages to the back. Before she reached the end, however, she landed upon a page with a frightening image. It was a large man with bright, wide eyes, kneeling in pitch-black darkness and eating a smaller man who hung lifeless and bloody in his hands. The giant's mouth was opened wide and a preparing to bite down again into the smaller man.

Faye couldn't look at the painting for long.

She quickly glanced at the title on the page beside it.

Chapter Thirteen: What It Feels Like To Die

It was then that Faye slammed the book shut. She was calmed by the idea of living forever over and over again, but she had forgotten that this still required her to actually die.

She didn't want to feel death.

She didn't want to be alone.

Faye slid the book under her bed and walked out of her room. She could hear the movie still playing downstairs, and for a moment she hesitated. Hurriedly, though, she continued on and ran her way down the stairs. She walked into the front room, which was dark and lit only by the blue light of the television screen. She sat beside her dad, and he wrapped his arm around her without saying a word. He was into the movie, and so was Claire, who sat at the other end of the couch. Faye was still terrified of what dying would feel like, but she was at least no longer alone, lying in her dad's arms. It was within them that she would fall asleep, disappearing into a dream of endless life and endless death.

The Ocean Of Others
Or, They

Oliver sat afloat in a sea of voices. His mind was half vanished, as it often was, from the world in which he did strange things to himself. Every few moments he would take a long drink from the green bottle in his hand, imbibing both expensive German beer and the liquid noise of people talking.

"Fuck," he said, yet no one heard him.

His bottle was empty and he wanted more.

He stood and walked his way into the kitchen. There he found Eric talking to some girl he didn't know.

"Hey," Oliver said, walking past them and to the fridge. He opened it wide and pulled out a bottle of beer that was sitting in a case marked OLIVER'S in large black letters. He turned and walked back to Eric and the girl.

"What's up, man?" Eric said, tossing him a bottle opener.

"Thanks," Oliver replied.

"Have you met Amber?" Eric asked, tilting his head to the girl beside him. She gave an awkward smile and waved, which Oliver thought was strange since she stood so close.

"Nope," he replied.

"Oh, well, this is Amber," Eric told him. "She works with Drew, but she's been around Moyenne for a little while now."

"Hello," Oliver said, slightly bowing to her with a smile.

"Hi," she said back, with a smile as well, before taking a drink from her red plastic cup.

"Oliver is a painter," Eric told her while walking to the nearby fridge to grab another drink of his own.

"Really?" she asked half-excitedly. Her dirty blonde hair fell over her face, and with her free hand she brushed it aside, rattling the metal bracelets she wore on her wrist.

"Yeah," Oliver replied, nodding his head. A brief awkwardness arose before he decided to continue on. "I'd like to get into it more, but with having to work full time it's hard to do."

"Oh, where do you work?" she asked.

"Ouro's" he answered. "I keep the place in one piece."

"The thrift store over on John Luke?"

"It's on Fifth actually, and it's more of a used book store with other shit. But yeah, you're probably thinking of the place"

"I've never been," she said, "but I'll have to go."

"Yup," Oliver replied.

"Have you seen Drew around?" Eric asked, stepping back into the conversation.

"Not since I've gotten here, actually," Oliver answered.

"He's probably off with Jess," he replied. "Wanna find him with me?" Eric asked, turning to Amber, who was taking quick sips from her drink. She nodded behind her red cup. "We'll be around," Eric said to Oliver, and he and Amber walked of into another part of the house.

Oliver strolled his way back to where he'd sat before. A person he only sort of knew, who he didn't feel comfortable talking to, now took up his seat, so he walked around the house instead, drinking his beer.

The half of his mind that hadn't yet vanished slowly began to fade away as well. The ethanol, which was a chemical drifting around in the beer that he drank, continued to work its way into his body. It coasted through his blood stream and to his brain, where it played games with his neurotransmitters. It slowed them down and made them disordered, which in turn slowed Oliver down and made him disordered. At first he forgot the little parts of himself that told him who he was and who he ought to be. The world became a little more vibrant, albeit a little more blurred.

His buried emotions began to grow from the alcohol playing with his limbic system. He wanted to scream out every feeling that arose in his head.

And lastly, the odd substance within his body teased his cerebellum, which made him bump into the walls as he walked down the hallway, looking for something, anything, to do.

He thought to himself about the people around him. He didn't especially like his generation. They were lazy, selfish, shallow, and stupid. He knew this wasn't a fair judgment and that there were probably still plenty of good people around, but he nevertheless couldn't help feeling that way. His generation spent all their time on the Internet, showing off their uneventful lives to other people who were too busy showing off their lives to even notice. And if they had to be away from their computers they stuck close to their cell phones. No one could be detached from their little devices for fear that something, somewhere, would happen that required them to know. This meant that the world in which they actually lived was lost, neglected, and slowly decaying.

Lots of people his age still lived at home with their parents. Many did nothing at all besides take from the world. Nobody seemed to give a damn anymore. Nobody seemed to look for anything deeper than the superficial life before them. Nobody read. Nobody took care of themselves. Nobody took care of the world around them. Oliver wondered if anybody even thought at all, or if they were just empty humans walking around, searching for food, fun, and a good fuck.

All of these thoughts spewed forth in his head, and most of them were twisted versions of a truth he really did believe in, a truth that was more compassionate and modest than the drunken feelings that overtook his mind. He didn't like his generation, but he didn't despise them. Humans are humans after all, and a human is something most certainly imperfect.

Besides, he thought, shouldn't their parents' generation be the ones to blame? They were the ones to raise them, shape them, and give to them a world that was quickly turning to shit.

Oliver snapped away from the blathering in his head and found himself standing in front of the house. He listened to the sea of sound behind him. He was done with the party, with these same old people doing the same old things. He wanted to be at home, alone with his thoughts. At this point, though, the alcohol was just beginning to have fun, and Oliver thought about Amber and how he wouldn't mind being alone with her.

"Nope," he said, pushing himself forward and somehow controlling his thoughts. He was done with drunken sex and pointless relationships. He wanted someone to actually love, and there was no one here for that.

"Hey, Oliver!" someone yelled out to him.

He turned and saw Drew walking across the lawn.

"You outta here?" Drew asked. "It's early as hell."

"Yeah," Oliver replied, unconsciously taking out a cigarette. "Tired. Good party though, man. Good party."

"Alright. See ya, then," Drew said, walking to his front door and stepping inside. As he did so a brief wave of unfiltered sound burst out of the house and cut through the night air.

"See ya," Oliver said before lighting up his cigarette.

He slowly walked his way home. His eyes burned from the cold wind. His lungs burned from the cigarette. And what was left of his mind burned with disgust at himself and everything and nothing at all.

Today
Or, Fragments

"So what do you think, Miss Radcliff?" Claire's teacher, Mr. Branson, asked her.

She hesitated, recollecting within seconds what was going on in class and formulating in her mind a hopeful answer to a guessed question. "I'd say *Brave New World* seems more likely," she answered, "but *1984* isn't impossible."

"M'kay," he said, walking to his podium and leaning his weight upon it. "Why do you think that?"

"You can see it happening around us right now," she replied, timidly at first, though gaining strength in her voice as she continued on. "We're always amusing ourselves and looking to have a good time. Eventually that's going to lead to the world Huxley wrote about. I mean, yes, we do have governments with surveillance everywhere, and political corruption, and wars being fought for power, but those wont stand a chance against our desire for pleasure. We all want to be entertained, to never grow old or experience pain, and, of course, to always be happy."

Mr. Branson gave a nod and rubbed his gray head of hair.

"Good answer. Good answer," he said, adjusting his glasses. "But don't you think your view on this is a bit skewed? You know the world through the eyes of citizen living in a prosperous nation. Imagine if you lived in a third world country or in a state where the government controlled your actions. Imagine if you'd never even seen a movie or listened to a CD or surfed the Internet. What would you think then?"

She thought for a moment and almost replied, but another student blurted out an answer.

"You'd think *1984* was closer to the truth."

"Maybe you would," Mr. Branson responded, "or maybe you wouldn't. There's no real answer here since everyone has his or her own opinion. The future is unknown. What matters is your belief and what you do to act upon it. If you fear an overpowering government, one that controls too much, then do your part to prevent that from happening. If you think our shallow desires to be entertained and happy will be our downfall, then stand up and work against those desires. That's what these kinds of books are about, getting you to think about what the future may hold if we don't tread very carefully in the present."

For a brief and seemingly rare moment Claire felt as if she had learned something from school. Most of the time she was in a daze, drifting through easy answers and pointless homework, getting by with As in most of her classes but never really thriving, always doing her minimal best.

But at this moment she felt she actually absorbed some sort of knowledge. She took the point her teacher was getting across and translated it into her own life. She had better start facing the present before it grew into a future she didn't want to live in. If she was unsatisfied with her life now, how would she feel in five, ten, fifteen years?

"Your tests will be this Thursday," Mr. Branson spoke out, "and after that, well, you can enjoy yourselves over the holiday. Just remember to stay away from the soma."

The class gave a few dull laughs, and as everyone began gathering up their things the school bell rang out over the speakers above. Claire stood from her desk and walked amongst the mass of students leaving the room. She walked down the hallway with her thoughts caught upon the idea that she would have to change her life right now. Tomorrow might be too late.

She reached her locker and opened it wide, gathering together her things and getting ready to leave.

"Thanks for making those posters, Claire," Megan said from behind her. She spun and met her friend standing close by.

"Oh, yeah, no problem," she replied.

"Do you wanna hang tonight?" Megan asked. "I've got nothing to do besides study, and that's not gonna happen."

"No, I can't," Claire answered, lifting her backpack over her shoulders. "I've got some things to do."

"Things to do?" Megan asked. "Like what? You're not hanging out with cheeseburger boy again, are you?"

"No. I've just got some stuff to get done."

"Whatever. We should at least do something this weekend. No more school for two weeks! Shit'll be awesome."

"I know, right? It's gonna be so nice."

"So we're hanging out Saturday then, and you can't say no."

"Okay, whatever."

"Good," Megan said, turning away and catching up with someone else she knew. "Later, Claire!" she shouted out.

"See ya," Claire replied, shutting her locker.

She walked down the hallway she had walked countless times before. With each step she felt an old identity falling away. She had decided to truly be herself before it was too late. She was going to change the present and become her own future.

But a thought came to her mind.

Just who was she anyway?

December 24th, 1986
Or, Then Comes Marriage

"Mia?" he asked again.

"Oh, sorry," she replied, turning to him and quickly blinking. "I was watching those kids over there." She pointed out of the car window directly toward the brightly setting sun. Arthur could just make out the nearly silhouetted shapes of four kids playing. They scurried about, swinging their arms at each other and dashing for a large ball they seemed to be fighting over.

One of them, a boy no older than eight or nine years, wore a long red cape that followed his every movement. In perfect moments, when the boy would move just right, the cape would catch the setting sun and glow a vibrant crimson as it fluttered behind his leaping body.

Arthur could see why Mia had been distracted. California had hardly put either of them in the Christmas mood, and there seemed to be within them a sort of longing for something that they couldn't quite explain. Their entire lives they had lived within the annual rhythm of the wintry holiday, and being in such a warm place during that time left them searching for the yearly emotion it produced.

The scene before them, the children playing in front of the golden sunset, seemed to evoke a feeling that, for Arthur at least, expressed the youthful sensation of Christmas. He didn't really understand why, but he knew that he felt it.

"Like a snowflake in the sand," he said, turning away from the setting sun and rubbing his eyes. He opened them to see Mia smiling. "What?" he asked, smiling back.

"I love you, Mr. Radcliff," she said, placing one hand on the back of his seat and the other gently on his knee.

"I love you too, Mrs. Radcliff," he replied.

They had only just married in September, but to the both of them it felt like they'd been together their whole lives.

In the middle of July, as Arthur sat alone on a park bench in the hot midday sun, he resolutely decided Mia was the one. Ever since the day they'd met nearly three years ago, Arthur felt as if he had found some missing part of himself, and he wanted that feeling of wholeness for the rest of his life. Within two days he bought a ring, and in three he got on one knee. As he stared up into her eyes, his heart nearly burst from joy when she happily cried yes. The two embraced beside a gentle willow tree, which Arthur had picked as the perfect place to ask the most important question of his life.

They got married two months later in the shade of that same tree, and two months after that they found themselves across the country in a California sunset.

"I need to finish the piece by Friday," Arthur said, reminding himself of his work and what needed to be done.

"Got it," Mia said, moving her hand away from his knee. "So everything's done?"

"Mostly, yes," he answered, wrapping his hands around the rubber of his steering wheel. "I still want to read over a few parts." He faintly smiled. "I at least know the photos are good."

"Oh, please," she replied, lifting her legs and placing her feet upon the dashboard. "Anyway, forget about that for now. It's Christmas Eve."

"You're right," he agreed, pushing his work out of his head.

Arthur had landed a job for another magazine, composing poetic articles about what it meant to be alive. He had been writing for them from across the country, but after he and Mia married they decided to move out West. In every issue the second-to-last page was his. He would write about various ordinary topics such as listening and driving and cooking dinner, but he would write about them in ways that gave reality a beautiful essence. The editor praised him for giving life such a heartfelt depth, even in the most mundane things. It seemed that his career as a writer was beginning to take shape.

Mia helped out by taking photographs for his articles, but she mostly worked at the small grocery store around the corner from their studio apartment. She would work during the day, as Arthur sat at his typewriter and wrote until she came home. In the evening they would love each other, and the world around them, until Arthur, on a few days out of the week, went to his night job, which was at the very same grocery store Mia worked at. The evenings he didn't work would be spent continuing their love until sleep pulled them apart.

Arthur started the car.

A Brian Eno cassette in the stereo came to life.

Gentle ambience filled their ears.

The sun was getting lower.

Its golden rays gave way to an airy blue of twilight.

Mia hummed to herself and then sighed.

"It was a good day," she said.

"It was," Arthur replied, nodding his head. "Let's go home. I've got a bottle of wine, a beautiful wife, and a Christmas tree to sit beside."

"Oh, so you'd like a good night too?" she asked as Arthur put the car in gear.

"As a matter of fact, I would," he said, driving away.

The Nothing Between Us
Or, Mute Words

"What do you think you'll get for Christmas, Faye?" asked Lucy, holding her backpack and swaying back and forth.

"I dunno," Faye answered. "Maybe a Wii. Or maybe some books. Or maybe clothes."

"A Wii?" Lucy replied, dropping her backpack to the floor. "You don't already have one?"

"No."

"Maybe you'll get one then."

"Yeah, maybe."

"I know I'll get clothes," Jessica added in.

"Me too," Lucy agreed.

The three girls were waiting for Jessica's mother to pick them up from school. It was their last day, and the three of them were going out for pizza with Jessica's parents to celebrate. Faye was excited to be off from school for a while. She wanted to sleep in and watch TV and play when she wanted to. She also needed the time to think about what had been bothering her so much lately.

"Do you guys know anything about dying?" she asked her friends, hoping they had information to share.

"Uhm," Lucy stuttered. "What?"

"Do you know anything about death?" Faye asked again.

Lucy stopped swaying back and forth and stood still. She seemed to be thinking about the question, and before she could answer Jessica spoke up.

"My grandpa died," she said. "He had cancer. It was weird."

"So, what happened to him?" Faye asked.

"He died," Jessica answered with a confused look.

"I mean, what happens when you die?" Faye pressed on.

"You go to heaven," Lucy rejoined.

"Yeah," Jessica agreed. "That's what my mom said too."

"So, like a place where everyone is happy?" Faye asked.

"In the clouds," Lucy told her, as Jessica moved to the window and strained to look outside.

"I dunno," Faye said. "What if there isn't a heaven?"

"But there is," Lucy said back.

"But what if there isn't?" Faye asked.

Lucy only shrugged her shoulders and resumed swaying back and forth. Jessica continued to stare out the window, and Faye stood silently thinking.

"I got my Dad a coffee mug for Christmas," Lucy said, changing the subject.

"Me too," Jessica said, jumping away from the window. "My mom's here. Let's go."

The three girls put on their backpacks and waited by the front doors, where their teacher, Mrs. Lawrence, was standing, handing out small gift bags of Christmas trinkets to the students as they left. Jessica's mother walked in through the doors, smiling to her daughter and her friends. She then spoke for a moment to their teacher, while the girls stood eagerly waiting to leave school behind. Finally, the two adults finished talking, and the three girls were led out into the cold, where they walked their way to the red minivan parked nearby.

Faye moved a little more slowly than the others, trailing just slightly behind. She wondered to herself about heaven and what it would be like. If it was happiness, she thought, then it would be forever with her family and her friends and her house and blue skies and warm weather.

Then she wondered if she believed in it or not.

She couldn't decide.

Like This
Or, Like That

Oliver watched his father fumble around with a large ball of knotted Christmas lights. The tangled strands of dark green wire clinked and clanged as the little glass bulbs upon them collided. Slowly, almost to the point of accomplishing nothing, his father unknotted the mess within his hands.

"These damn lights," he said, tugging at a loop of wire that had come free from the clutter. "Every year I do this. Every damn year. When I put them away I make sure they're nice and organized, but when I take them out I always have to unravel this mess." He pulled at another string of lights, which seemed to make the tangled heap knot itself into an even worse clutter. "Every damn year."

"Well," Oliver said, fiddling with a dusty box of decorations that sat in his father's garage, "maybe you should just leave the lights up year-round. Then you wouldn't have to worry about it anymore."

"That would be nice," his father replied, keeping most of his attention upon the mess in his hands and not on what had been said.

Oliver lost interest in the box of decorations and began to wander about the garage, looking around at old heaps of things he had seen countless times before. Eventually he stood beside his father's motorcycle, which sat in the one organized corner of the garage. He lifted his leg over and sat upon the seat. His hands rested on the handlebars, and for a moment he felt he was someone else.

"Forget it," his father said, tossing the ball of Christmas lights down. "I'll deal with it tomorrow."

"Didn't Jeanne want them up by today?" Oliver asked.

"Yeah. And Faye too," he answered, walking over to Oliver and the motorcycle. "But they'll have to settle with tomorrow."

"You know Christmas is next week," Oliver said. "Don't you usually have those up by the first of December?"

"It's been a busy month," his father replied, gesturing him off of the bike with a nod of his head. Oliver climbed off and moved a few steps back. He rested against the small worktable behind him.

"Teaching?" Oliver asked. "Or writing?"

"Both," his father answered, climbing onto the motorcycle. He sat for a moment with one hand on the handlebars, rubbing his closed eyes with the other. "I've got a lot of students this semester. And I'm halfway through my book. Between the two of them I'm drained." He turned to Oliver. "How about you? How's work going?"

"It's good," he replied, pushing his hands into the pockets of his jacket. "I'm working a lot of hours. And they're paying me pretty well. I'm the one holding the place together half the time."

"That's good. Though just wait until you slave away all day and then come home to a house full of children. Then you'll really know what it means to work."

"Yeah, I can only imagine."

"How's painting coming? That's what really matters."

Oliver hesitated for a moment. He wasn't sure how to answer. He was fairly proud of the work he had done, but as for how well he was doing outside of his own judgment, he was failing.

"It's okay," he said, shrugging his shoulders.

"Okay?" his father asked, stepping off the motorcycle and standing beside it.

"Yeah, I mean, I'm still painting. And I'm painting okay stuff. But I haven't really gotten anywhere."

"You really sound like you've got a passion for it, Oliver," his father said sarcastically.

"Thanks," Oliver replied, sarcastically as well.

"If you really want to do this, then you've got to really try."

"I know, I know. It's just hard sometimes."

"Yes, it is. I've been there. But when the going gets tough."

"The tough get going," Oliver finished with a half-smile.

"Speaking of," his father said, "I think I'm gonna get to work writing. It's not often I get the time to. You're welcome to hang around here. Jeanne's coming by later. You can have dinner with us?"

"Oh, no, it's okay," Oliver replied. "I suppose I've got some work to do too."

"You're still on for Christmas, right?" his father asked.

"Of course," he answered, nodding his head.

"Good," his father said, stepping closer and hugging him. "Take it easy, Oliver."

"I will," he said as they let go.

Oliver walked out through the side garage door and into the chill air. The day had been mostly gray, but now that the sun had begun to set the sky had changed into a pale ashen blue. Hints of pink shined across the farthest clouds, and a hazy orange burned along the horizon.

Reality hung close to Oliver as he walked down the dry, snowless sidewalk. The ordinary world around him seeped deep into his skin, and he felt trapped within the normality of everything. This was a common occurrence for him, one that at first made his soul burn for passionate change, but now it merely made him want to escape into nothing, forgetting the world and forgetting himself.

But what was reality anyway?

The question bothered him. He had tried to define reality countless times before. All that he could ever come up with was this—the life right in front of him. But his mind wouldn't let that answer be. Why should his view of existence be the definitive answer? He was just another human amongst billions, perceiving the world with the few senses he possessed. There could be, and mostly likely was, so much more than he could observe. But how could he know if all that he knew was this? Hence, the life before him was his reality.

Still, an incessant thought bothered him. How could all of existence be nothing other than the mundanity around him? Something amazing had to lie beneath it all. His desire-driven reason told him so. Why would anything exist if its existence was governed by some separate rationality? Wouldn't God, or whatever it was that was everything, want to be in control of the sublime?

Oliver believed in the incredible, not the everyday, for the vastness of simply being demanded extraordinariness.

Yet, regardless, he was a part of the mundane, and even if there was more to existence than what he saw, it had nothing to do with him. His life was here and now within the physical world. He knew this because science, and his own experience of life, told him so, and to deny science, and his own experience, would be to deny reason. It was only logical to believe in scientific fact, to believe in the laws of nature, to believe in cause and effect.

Or did logic lead to something deeper, something vague?

To Oliver, it was logical to believe in an existence that was eternal and infinite in possibilities. The only problem was he didn't know why it was logical to believe so. Perhaps it wasn't even rational at all. In fact, maybe it was the opposite, a hopeful emotion disguised in reason. But he nonetheless believed it was the truth, which pushed him deeper into looking for an answer beyond the world in which he lived.

Oliver stopped beside an empty lot. Tall dead grass and patches of mud scattered the abandoned area. Two sad-looking trees sat amongst the small, barren landscape, and their branches glowed eerily in the cloudy sunset.

Oliver stared down at his right hand, which he held close to his face. He stared at the skin of his palm and tried to see the truth.

He looked.

And he looked.

Yet all that he saw was the flesh of a human being.

He tried to forget that he was looking at his hand. He tried to just see what was there in front of his eyes. For a moment he thought he glimpsed something beneath it all, but it quickly faded back into the skin of his hand.

He gave up and walked forward. The air had become colder, and his breath was making large clouds of vapor every time he exhaled.

Maybe, he thought, there was no such thing as reality?

In fact, he decided that was the most logical answer. Reality was just an empty name for an empty idea. All that really existed was existence, and it didn't really exist at all.

If this were true, where did his being fit into the void? Was life a way of giving shape to the shapeless? Did we create our worlds within the endless unreality of reality?

Oliver wondered about other people's lives and how they affected his own. Was it their interaction that created existence? After all, everyone seemed to live within the same old reality. People agreed upon what was true, and that was that. But other people would often come along, and they would see the gaps in between the shared lies. Reality would crumble away into a new way of being. Over and over again, people created the world and tore it down, and they could do this because there was no real substance behind their lives in the first place. These artificial realities were molded by the way people communicated, and the way people communicated changed over time. In the past, humans talked much closer to reality, or rather unreality, and so they shared something a little more near to the emptiness beneath it all. But as time moved on, people found new ways of interacting. They began to write books, take pictures, make movies, play games, and surf the Internet. Interactions moved away from the shared emptiness of life and into the false sense of being someone somewhere doing something.

Oliver knew who controlled the world. He saw it as he walked down the average streets of Moyenne. It was in the crumpled up soda bottle sitting in the gutter, in the bright bold letters of a billboard, in the cars that quickly drove past. It was even in his own thoughts, placed there by a life lived inside the machine. It was business that held reality. In this world, the one that humans had created, buying and selling were God.

People watched TV, unknowingly letting it mold their minds. People went to the movies, allowing the stories before them to shape their thoughts. They read books and magazines and advertisements, falling into the ideas that were pushed into their heads. No one wanted to admit that the world was one big make believe story, so everyone just played along, following the rules that somebody else made. It was nearly impossible to face the harsh fact that there was no reality saying you had to have a job, or drive a car, or get married, or wear clothes, or even stay alive. You had to play the game just to keep your sanity, or at least that was one of the rules of the reality humans played.

To simply live within the world, to return to the unreal, was what Oliver wanted. More than that, he desired to show others the way. All of humanity should aspire for the truth.

He laughed at himself for thinking so.

What way would he show? The only path he had ever followed was the same one everyone else took. He was just another person, living his life day to day. He had as many problems as the next guy, and he was failing at doing anything to solve them.

He stood in front of the door to his apartment, staring at his existence. He unlocked the door and walked in, away from his thoughts and into a familiar escape.

From There To Here To There
Or, The Center Of Yourself

She didn't need this.

Or that.

Or any of it, really.

All she needed was herself.

And that was something she didn't have.

Claire tossed an old notebook into the large cardboard box beside her. It fell atop the mound of odds and ends already inside, the pictures of friends she no longer cared for, the plush animals that somehow stuck around through time, the poster of a sexy TV vampire, the red and blue track and field ribbons, the badly painted rock that looked like a lion, the cheap necklace her first boyfriend had gotten her from a bubblegum machine, the shiny folders of neon-colored kittens in neon-colored places, and her collection of miniature horse figures, which she stopped collecting years ago but still had sitting neatly aligned upon the windowsill in her room.

Claire saw empty reflections of an old self in everything around her. She felt like a ghost, dead to this life and searching for another. The only belongings left in her room were the things that breached the void between past and future. In other words, she held onto what could still somehow speak, through deep emotions and hidden meaning, to the phantom that was her present state of life.

Objects from her mother remained, like the metal bracelet she wore every day, inscribed in copper with a Buddhist prayer, or the film camera she used back before Claire, or even Oliver, was born. The shoebox of old family photos stayed too. Claire spent some time gazing at them, feeling a muted sadness for the past, yet also a quiet happiness for the memories she possessed. She stared at a younger version of herself in pale film colors holding an infant Faye and looking happily terrified. There was the photo of little Oliver smiling in the bright sunshine of a beach, and behind him was an even younger form of herself playing in the sand. The oldest photo was of her father and mother, holding hands and smiling, posing beside a willow tree after they had gotten married. The colors were faded and the edges were blurred, but Claire loved the way it made the picture feel, like a real memory in all its vagueness pulled from someone's head. Her mother looked so beautiful, with her long dark hair, her slender body, and her smiling eyes. Claire hoped she would someday have that same beauty, the kind that was more than skin deep, yet nevertheless revealed itself through an outward attractiveness.

Claire's books still stood upon her shelf, though a few of them she did toss into the box of her past. Her dresser was still covered in half-melted candles. Upon her desk remained the wooden jewelry box she had gotten for her birthday from her father last year. She started to look through it, but stopped out of boredom.

She was done with getting rid of her past. It was all just stuff anyway. What really needed to change, she thought, was what was inside of her. She fell face down upon her bed and breathed in and out the moist warm air that barely left her lungs. Eventually she turned over for want of fresh air. She stared at the blank white ceiling and wondered what to do with herself.

How could she change the life she lived? She tried to define what it was that she didn't like about herself, which came out to be her apathy, her passiveness, and, in her mind, her lack of any talent. She decided to become more passionate about life, which she felt she was already doing, seeing as she was in her current state of transformation. She would also have to stand up for her beliefs more. That seemed easy enough, though she did doubt whether or not she would stand her ground once she was around her friends and classmates. And finally, she would have to find something to be good at. This, she believed, would be the hardest of all. Where would she begin? She wasn't good, or bad, at anything. She was just somewhere in the middle of it all.

In the middle of it all.

The words bounced around in her head and settled down deep into her mind. That was it, she thought. Exactly it. She was in the middle of everything. She was that single empty point at the center of the universe. She was nowhere, and she could go in any direction, become anything she wanted. But until she did so, she would remain within that little, vacant, indistinct point that had become her life.

December 24th, 1988

Or, Then Comes The Creation Of Life

Arthur stared into his son's eyes.

They looked back in a way that he had never seen before.

It was as if the entire universe was staring back at him, seeing with its two small eyes the world from which it came and the world to which it would become. Within this little human being there was the immensity of everything gazing at itself for the very first time.

Arthur's contemplation of his son, as well the universe, was cut short by the fear that now haunted him nearly every second of his life.

When Mia told him she was pregnant he most certainly felt fear, alongside joy and wonder and exhilaration, but it wasn't the same fear that he felt now. As he watched his wife's belly grow he felt fear for the future, but it was nothing compared to the anxiety he faced when finally there. And when she was going into labor he felt a nervousness stronger than any he had ever known, yet still it was pale in comparison to the fear that he now faced every day of his fatherly life.

The moment Oliver was born, Arthur felt the fear of infinite responsibility. In his hands was a fragile life, one which he and his wife created, living in the cruel and dangerous world of reality. It was Arthur's duty as a parent to care for that delicate existence above all else, even his own life.

Before Oliver was born, Arthur's main concern about being a father was whether or not his self-centered mind would allow another life to supersede his own. What about his goals? What about his own adventures? Could he really settle down and work away his soul just to feed and clothe and shelter a child?

Now that he held his son in his hands, Arthur no longer questioned if he could give his all. He instead wondered if his all would be enough. Could he protect Oliver from the world around him, from the dangers of merely being alive in a universe that was mostly dead? And, over the years, could he guide that growing soul through the strange, mundane, beautiful, painful, joyous, and, above all else, absurd existence of human life?

"Look at you," Arthur's mother said, standing in the doorway across the room. "I can't believe my little boy is a father." She walked closer, tilting her head down at Oliver. "And the father of such a beautiful child as him. Look at those eyes."

"I can't believe it either, to tell you the truth," Arthur replied with a heartfelt smile on his lips.

"Oh, you'll be fine," she said, gently sliding her hands around Oliver and pulling him close. She held him in her arms and gently swayed back and forth. "By the third one you'll be changing diapers in your sleep."

"Third?" Arthur cut back. "I think one will do. Besides, it did for you, didn't it?"

"Well, you were so unique that you counted as three kids all by yourself," she replied. "And besides, I knew you'd give me lots of little grandchildren to care for."

"Lots of grandchildren?" Mia asked, walking into the living room with her father-in-law at her side.

"Yes, apparently we're to have lots children, just so my mom will be happy." Arthur said, grinning.

"It's the least you can do for me," his mother said, looking to Mia with playful, yet sincere, eyes. "After all, I did bring the man you love into this world."

"Well, you didn't do that alone." Arthur's father said, walking across the room and slowly sitting down upon his large reclining chair.

"Yes, yes," his mother replied, "but you didn't have to push him and that big head of his out of your body."

He ignored her remark and reached for the remote control that sat beside him on the coffee table. With it he turned on the television. It came to life with a screen of static and a low hum that invaded the room.

"This damn antenna," he said, standing up with a grunt. He walked to the television, and the rough short hairs on his face began to glow as he approached the bright TV. He twiddled with the two antennas, watching in hopes of an image coming upon the screen.

"Frank was just showing me the new CD player in the family room," Mia said, walking over to Arthur.

"I've got Doris Day, Elvis Presley, The Everly Brothers, and a few more," his father said, still twisting about the TV antennas. "Its like they're right there in the room, singing to you. Forget that old record player."

"Wow," Arthur said, looking to his mother. "I didn't think I'd see the day when Dad not only owned a CD player but actually enjoyed it."

The static upon the TV screen finally gave way to the image of Charlie Brown and Linus walking through a multitude of colorful aluminum Christmas trees.

"There," his father said, moving back to his chair.

"Well, who gets the baby?" Arthur's mother asked, offering little Oliver to either one of his parents. "I've got to get back to dinner."

"I'll take him," Mia said with a smile, softly taking her son and holding him close.

Arthur watched the two of them together.

He stood in complete wonder at what he had in his life.

The woman he loved, the one who he would do anything at all for, had become the mother to his child. His life was now no longer his own, and it felt surprisingly good to have let that weight go. He now had another, larger, burden to bear, but to him it felt lighter than air. It was the strength his family gave him that made the heavy task so easy. Just watching Oliver and Mia together was enough reason for him to carry the entire world upon his shoulders.

She looked to him and smiled, her dark hair falling over the side of her face. Arthur felt the desire he always did when she showed herself to him through her subtle, beautiful way of living.

Oliver made a small yawn, stretching his arms through the soft, blue blanket around him. Arthur moved next to his wife and child, feeling the love and warmth of his family. This is life, he thought.

"*That's what Christmas is all about, Charlie Brown,*" said Linus upon the television, and tender jazz piano played across the room.

With My Very Own Eyes
Or, The Only Way To Sort Of Know

Faye stood in the snow, looking for death.

She wasn't really sure where to look.

She had never seen death before.

Where had it been hiding all her life?

She stepped forward through the shallow white layer at her feet. Staring down, she watched as her steps left dark green imprints behind where the cold, damp grass broke through.

She walked along until she stood before the black chain-link fence that separated her family's backyard from the alley that ran behind it. In warmer months a large leafy vine grew along the fence, but during the winter most of its leaves fell off and left behind a sad-looking branch that twisted itself across the chain-linked metal.

Faye supposed that its leaves must be dead, but as she stared at them she saw nothing she hadn't seen before. She picked one of the thin, lifeless, brown leaves that still hung from the vine and held it close to her face. It was dead all right, but it was hard for her to sympathize with a dead leaf. It was too different from the life she knew. Plants didn't talk, or play, or, though she wasn't completely sure about it, think or feel at all. She even ate plants, which was something she certainly wouldn't do to a living thing like herself.

She took a step back and kicked a cloud of snow towards the fence for no other reason than to see it happen. Afterwards she crumbled the dead leaf in her hands and watched as the dark brown leaf scattered across the bright white snow.

Faye wished she could leave the backyard, since she didn't think she would find much death in the confines of it, but her dad wouldn't let her, and she didn't dare do what he told her not to. So she stood cold for a moment, trying think of where she could find death in such a small, safe place.

She decided a bug would be her only chance. They were everywhere, and they were living things, so they must die too. Maybe somewhere along the side of the house, where the bushes grew, she could find some insects that had survived the winter cold.

Faye ran to one of the thick green shrubs and kicked away some of the snow that sat beside it. There she knelt down and tried to look into the darkness beneath the bush. She couldn't see much from where she was. She would have to crawl under it if she were to see anything at all.

It was at this point that she had doubts about what she was doing. Did she really want to see death? Shouldn't it be something she should avoid? She also disliked the idea of crawling in the cold dirt and getting so close to whatever nasty creatures lived beneath the bushes.

But Faye resolved to stick with her plan. She would need to know death firsthand if she were to really understand it. She pulled up the hood of her winter coat and grudgingly began to crawl her way through the underside of the bush. Her gloves became damp and cold in the mud, and the stiff branches of the shrub kept jabbing at her body. She stopped crawling after a couple feet or so, and she found herself in a small sort of dome that rested between the bush through which she had entered and the one beside it. The air smelled of cold pine and wet earth, and all Faye could hear was the muffled sound of the wind blowing against the thick shrubs she was within. In front of her sat the dirty yellow siding of the house where it met the thick layer of gray bricks beneath it. The ground was a mixture of dark, moist dirt and scattered layers of bronze pine needles. Everywhere else around her was the deep green of the shrubs. Small patches of white, from both the sky outside and the snow that sat upon the bristly leaves, scattered the otherwise dark place she was in.

"There," she blurted out to herself. Some sort of bug was crawling along the ground about a foot from her face. It was a rather boring-looking bug, and she couldn't really tell what it was. It seemed like a mixture of a beetle, a cockroach, and an ant. All in all it was just a small reddish-brown thing that awkwardly walked along the frozen ground.

So now what was she to do? Follow it around until it died? She didn't want to lie in the cold that long. If she really wanted to see it die, she would have to kill it herself. It wouldn't be the first time she killed a bug. Once, out of instinct, she smashed an ant that was crawling along her arm. It smeared brown guts across her skin, which grossed her out, but at the time she didn't really comprehend what she had done. She was too young to realize death was a thing. She even smashed a bug in the hallway of her house once, but then, too, she didn't think of it as killing. She was protecting herself from it, and nothing more.

Now, however, she believed she was smart enough to know what life was truly like. And knowing that, she couldn't muster the nastiness to kill the bug in front of her. It was minding its own business, living its own life, and what right did she have to kill it? In fact, it seemed outright evil for her to do so.

Faye was tired of being crammed into the dirt beneath the bushes, so she gave up her search and crawled her way back out into the bright white of the day.

Maybe death wasn't as common as she thought. Maybe it was a rare and hidden thing that, if she were lucky, she wouldn't have to face. The world couldn't be so bad that things just up and died left and right. But then again, as her book had told her, if something was alive, it had to die. And when she thought about it, there were lots and lots of things that were alive.

Faye walked across the snow to the back door of her house. She felt a strange disappointment about not being able to see something die, and she couldn't understand why she couldn't stop thinking about death.

Things Are What You Make Of Them
Or, Morning Canvas

"I don't know," Oliver said, sitting at the table and resting his cheek upon his closed hand. He took a sip from the straw that sat in his smoothie. Michelle had made the drink for him shortly after he came by. It was morning, and he had to work later, but he had wanted to stop in to see her and Mike and Audrey. Something about being around parents that were nearly his own age made him feel more secure about life. "I mean, what am I supposed to do with my art?" he asked. "Who the hell makes money off painting these days?" He took another drink. "This is great by the way, really."

"Thanks," Michelle replied. "It's got a little bit of everything in it." She sat down across from him at the table. "And to be honest, not many people make money off painting. But that's not why you paint, now is it?"

"No, it's not," he answered, "but I'd like to make money in a way that doesn't grind me to a pulp. I'd like to be successful."

"And what does that mean?"

"It means I'd like to be successful."

She took a long drink from the straw in her smoothie, and all the while she stared up into his eyes with a playful look of scorn.

"Okay," he said in reply. "I'd like to make art that expresses whatever the hell it is I want to express. And that's something that changes. I want to paint the truth I see, as well as the lies. I want to show the beauty within and without, and the ugliness that's in the same damn place. I want to create sincere pieces of art. And if I do that, I'd like to think that whatever it is I made was pretty good, and that other people would like it as well."

"Now that's a better answer," she said, smiling. "But why do you need money then?"

"Oh, come on. We're both hippies here, Michelle, but let's not lie about life. We need money. We live in a world that runs on money. I'm not saying that I agree with that world, or that I want to cooperate with it, but the only way out of it is to control what runs the damn thing in the first place. I say let's all get rich and tear this shit hole down. Fight fire with fire, because at this point water won't do a damn thing to stop the flames."

"You know, you're a different person every five minutes."

"What?"

"Well, sometimes you're quiet little Oliver, just minding his own business and zoning out. And other times you have something to say, and you'll say it damn proud. And then there's all the other Olivers. The depressed one, the happy one, the drunk one, the high one, the young one, the old, and of course, the one you are right now."

"Which one is that?"

"The fake one."

"What? Fake?"

"Yes, the fake one."

"But I just told you what I want! Now I'm fake?"

"Yes, because that's not what you believe in."

"Oh, then what do I believe in?"

"Nothing."

"Nothing?" he asked, picking up his drink and leaning back in his chair. She silently nodded at him. "Why nothing?" he asked after gulping down the pink smoothie in his hand. "And how do you know?"

"Because you've told me the millions of times you've either gotten drunk or stoned. And secondly, because I know you, Oliver, and you're too unique to believe in anything."

"Wait, so believing in something is bad?"

"No, not bad," she answered, shaking her head. She brushed aside her hair, and the large earrings she wore jangled as she did. She crossed her arms and seemed to be mimicking Oliver's posture. "For a lot of people believing in something is good. And for many others it's awful. Think about all the stuff that happens, all the good or bad. Most of it happens because of people's beliefs. But few and far between there's the sort of people that just don't believe in a thing. And I'm not talking about some nihilistic, depressing sort of belief in nothing, or an apathetic, passive, don't give a damn about the world belief in nothing." She let her arms down and leaned forward onto the table. She gave a small smile and looked him in the eyes. At this point Oliver felt affection for Michelle, for the way she spoke and the thoughts she had and the beautiful way in which she carried herself. It was something that often happened, but it was something he easily brushed aside out of love and respect for his friend Mike. Besides, he valued Michelle just as she was, a good friend, and he knew his brief infatuations for her were simple feelings of attraction and nothing more. "I'm talking about people like you, Oliver," she continued. "People that believe in nothing with all their soul."

"I don't get it," he replied.

"You believe in nothing. And I mean no-thing. Nada. Some people believe in nothing like it's a something, and go about saying life is nothing when they mean it's something. But people like you can see the real emptiness in everything, you know? And you can see it for what it is. It's zilch. It's not there! That's what life is. It's emptiness, and that's the nothing that you believe in. People that know that live like no other. They're free from everything, yet so in tune with life that you can just feel it when you're around them. They can see there's no meaning or meaninglessness. Everything just is, and that's it. There are no words to muddle it up. It just is. And that's what you believe in. Not some ideology, or art form, or religion, or philosophy, or way of life. What you believe in is nothing."

Oliver shook his head and rubbed his eyes.

"You may have lost me there," he replied, "but you also just might have found me out."

"Exactly!" she laughed, grabbing her smoothie and taking a drink, smiling the whole time. Oliver nodded his head as if in contemplation, but in truth he didn't know what to think. Was she right?

"You're living in a world where everyone has to believe in something," Michelle continued in a softer voice, stopping Oliver's thoughts. "So you make up some sort of belief that seems nice to you. And in truth, they're not bad beliefs, but they're not really yours. So stop thinking about it and just be who you really are."

He knew that she was right.

"So what am I supposed to do if I don't believe in anything?"

"I dunno," she answered. "Nothing, or something, or whatever you want. You're the one who believes in nothing, not me."

"You know," he said, standing from his seat. "Even if I don't believe in anything, I'd still like to make some money."

"Sell your paintings then!" she said, standing too.

"To who?" he asked.

"People who believe in paintings," she replied.

"Audrey!" Mike yelled out from across the house.

"Audrey!" Michelle yelled in repeat, sensing the tone in Mike's voice and knowing what it was he was yelling about. Just then, their daughter Audrey quickly ran past, laughing a high-pitched laugh and wearing nothing other than a shiny yellow rain hat.

"Audrey!" Michelle shouted again, chasing after her.

The three-year-old darted for the doorway, but there she was met by her father, who grabbed her up and wrapped his arms around her. To this, she began to cry.

"Don't mind us," Mike said to Oliver. "It's just bath time, and our little nudist likes to run free whenever she gets the chance." He carried his daughter out of the room, and Michelle gave a small laugh mixed with a sigh. She turned to Oliver, who was smiling.

"That," she told him, "is what I believe in."

"Family?" he asked.

She shook her head no.

"Just love."

Through The Middle
Or, To The Edge

"So what does your bracelet mean?" Megan asked.

"Huh?" Claire replied, not hearing the question. She was lost in thought and blankly staring at the seafoam green brick wall of the school cafeteria.

"Your bracelet," Megan asked again, "what does it say?"

"Oh, it's Sanskrit," she answered. Claire had started wearing her mother's bracelet, a decision that she made while lying in bed and dreaming of the life she wanted to live. Maybe it would bring her some guidance, she thought. In a way it made her feel connected to a past buried deep within her body and mind, yet at the same time it was a reminder of the future self she wanted to become. "It says Om Mani Padme Hum."

"What's that mean?" Megan asked, looking uninterested.

"I don't think it really has a meaning," Claire answered. She remembered her father telling her so when he gave her the bracelet many years back. He said that it literally translated into something along the lines of following the right path to reach enlightenment, but that the real meaning was more in the sound of the words than the words themselves. She didn't want to try and explain this to her friend, so she left her answer at that.

"Oh, okay." Megan replied. "I like it. Where'd you get it?"

"It used to be my mom's."

"Oh, well, it's nice."

"Thanks."

That was the end of the conversation. The two of them sat quietly waiting for school to begin. It was the final day before the holidays, and their classes were either going to be full of tests to take or, if they had already done so, wastes of time.

"Hey," Madison said, sitting next to them. Claire didn't really consider her a friend, but she wasn't an enemy either. She was just there, like so many of her classmates. They were people that pervaded Claire's daily life and shaped the world around her, but once they all graduated she would never see or think of them again.

"I am so ready to get outta here," Madison said, tossing her backpack onto the table in front of them.

"Me too," Megan groaned back. "Me too for sure. This damn place is killing me."

"Killing you?" Madison replied. "At least you don't have to face your ex in every class today."

"Shut the fuck up," Megan said back in a quiet, yet thrilled, voice. "Jason is in all of your classes?"

Madison shook her head yes and rolled her eyes.

"I'm gonna head to class," Claire said, standing up. "It's ten till. You guys have fun today."

"Oh, you know it," Megan told her, and Madison gave a slight laugh. Claire walked her way out of the lunchroom and down the hall to her locker. She undid the lock, opened the door, and tossed her backpack inside. She needed nothing for her first class other than a pencil and the willpower to stay awake.

The sun had just begun to rise, and the sky outside was a dark cold blue. Its light dimly shone through the windows, flooding the hallways with the feeling of drowsiness. Everyone around Claire seemed to be half awake, though she sensed the oncoming day slowly stirring within the walls. Soon the building would be full of teenagers who were about to be out of school for two weeks, which meant soon the building would be full of noise and energy and, to Claire, annoyances.

No, no, no, she thought to herself. This wasn't who she wanted to be. She didn't want to be a cynical person. She didn't want to be depressed. She just wanted to be herself. But wasn't she already? She wasn't trying to be cynical. That's just how she was.

Why did being herself make her feel so down? Was it because she wasn't really herself yet? Or was it because she didn't belong here? Was her true calling somewhere else out there in the world?

Om Mani Padme Hum.

She said the words in her head.

And she realized that who she was wasn't dependent upon where she was. If she were to be herself, she would have to do so in the face of whatever the world gave her.

Om Mani Padme Hum.

She said the words over and over again, slowly moving them from her mind and out into the world, at first through silent lips and then in faint whispers.

Om Mani Padme Hum.

Who was she?

Om Mani Padme Hum.

Where was she?

Om Mani Padme Hum.

Why was she?

December 24th, 1995
Or, Love Within Your Words

Arthur watched his wife making food for their children, and he realized, as she stood there stirring pots of food upon the stove, that she nearly looked like a completely different person than the woman he had married years ago. This was only reasonable, he thought, since so much time had passed since then and having had two children along the way. But still, she looked so unlike the Mia he married nine years ago or, even more so, the Mia he first fell in love with on a burnt October day.

It wasn't that she looked particularly aged. She was only thirty-one years old, and Arthur still thought she was the most beautiful woman he had ever seen. But something about the way she carried herself had changed. The way her eyes looked at the world seemed different from before. They weren't yet jaded, but they no longer displayed the outward wonder that they did in the past. They now carried an acceptance of the inevitable difficulties they would see, and along with that acceptance came a layer of heavy fatigue. Her hair was different too. She had dyed it dirty blonde and cut it short, so that it stopped just as it met the skin of her neck. And her skin, Arthur realized, had changed as well. It wasn't as smooth as it used to be, but it now had a richness to it that radiated the life within her.

He looked down at his own hands and wondered how much he had changed too. He had turned thirty-five this year and had been blessed with his second child. He worked practically all the time, raising his children during the day and writing his book at night. He drank too much coffee and ate too much food, giving him a slight belly and a daily case of heartburn.

Arthur could plainly see, looking down at his hands, that his skin had changed as well. His didn't posses the radiance of a difficult life lived in elegance, like that of his wife's, but rather the eroding of a life plowed through in endless contemplation. He knew that being a writer would be demanding, but he followed that path nonetheless. Finding an income wasn't the most challenging aspect, though it too brought its fair share of trouble. Rather, it was the ceaseless rambling that went on in his head. He was unable to stop thinking for one peaceful second. He lived within a world of words, and he had to know those words well, learning the letters that spelled out his existence and organizing them into beauty lined upon a page. His life was an endless story to be read and contemplated.

"Arthur," Mia said from the kitchen.

"Yes?" he replied.

"The food is almost done. Could you get the kids ready?"

"Sure," he answered, turning to look at Claire sitting upon the floor. She was playing with large, soft blocks, swinging them around in front of herself. Each side of the blocks had different pictures of animals on them. She stopped swinging one and held it still, looking perplexedly at the image of a lion. Arthur moved down to the floor and sat beside her.

"That's a lion," he said, pointing to the drawing on the side of the block. "Liiiiiooooooonnnn," he slowly repeated, in the hope that she could understand.

"Ehwn!" Claire grunted back, moving the block to her mouth and gnawing on its soft corner.

"Oh, come on," Arthur said, pulling the cube from her mouth. "Don't do that." He turned the block about until it showed a dog. Maybe it would be an easier word to say. "Dog," he told his daughter. "Doooog."

She looked at the picture and then to him.

"Ehwn," she mumbled back, trying to grab the block from his hands. He laughed and brushed the soft hair upon her head.

"C'mon," lets get you ready. He lifted her up and walked her to the kitchen, where he placed her into her high chair.

"I'll be right back," Arthur told Mia. He walked into the hallway and to Oliver's room. He knocked on the open door before walking in. "It's time for dinner."

"I'm almost done," Oliver answered, sitting on the floor and playing a video game.

"What're you playing?" Arthur asked, walking closer and standing beside his son.

"*StarTropics*," the boy blankly replied.

"Oh, that's a good one," Arthur said back, "but you're gonna have to stop. It's Christmas Eve, you know? And we're going to have a good dinner together. Then it's bed. After all, Santa is coming tonight."

Oliver paused his game and turned to give Arthur a strange look. He began to say something, but hesitated.

"Can I save it first?" he mumbled out. "I'm almost there."

"Okay" Arthur replied. "But you've got five minutes. And put on a nice shirt for your mother."

Oliver unpaused his game and went back to playing without a word. Arthur turned and walked from the room, heading back into the hallway. From where he was standing he could see Claire sitting in her high chair. She had a sour look upon her face, one which Arthur knew well. He rubbed his eyes and walked to the kitchen, and when he reached it Claire let out a piercing wail.

"She's hungry!" Mia gently shouted, scrambling around the kitchen. Arthur moved to his daughter and lifted her from her seat. He hushed into her ear and softly rubbed her back. Still, she kept crying.

"I think Claire gets to eat before us," he said to his wife.

"Yes, yes she does," Mia replied, setting a bowl of mashed peas and potatoes onto the little table attached to Claire's highchair. Arthur continued to pat his daughter on the back until the crying faded into quiet sobs. He placed her back down and sat beside her.

"Oliver will be here in a minute, or at least he better be," he said to Mia. "I'll feed her for now if you want to change or something."

"Change?" she asked, "Why do I need to change?"

"You don't need to," he said, spooning a small dollop of potatoes into Claire's mouth. "I just thought you might want to."

"Mmhm," Mia replied with a tender scorn. She walked out of the room, and, soon after, Oliver wandered in. He sat in his chair and looked vacantly forward at the table.

"Did you save your game?" Arthur asked.

"Yeah," Oliver answered. "What's for dinner?"

"I dunno. Your mother made it. I think mashed potatoes, and salad, and pasta with beans or something like that."

"Okay. Where's Mom?"

"She's getting changed, I think."

There was a brief pause, and the only sound Arthur heard was the Christmas music coming from the living room stereo.

"So if Santa wasn't real would I still get presents?" Oliver asked out of nowhere.

"Why do you think he isn't real?" Arthur replied hesitantly.

"Because I'm seven years old," his son answered. "And it just doesn't make sense. How could he do what he does? Flying around the world and giving everyone presents. Also, a few kids have talked about it at school, and they said he wasn't."

"Well," Arthur said, pausing for a moment to think. "To be honest, he isn't real. It's something parents do for their children." He looked Oliver in the eyes, believing now would be the right time for his son to find out. "It's fun to believe in Santa Claus. It gives children lots of happiness, and their parents too. Just because he isn't real doesn't mean you have to forget him. Think of Santa as the spirit of Christmas. He may not be the one bringing you presents, but he does an awfully good job of getting people in the holiday spirit."

Oliver gave a look of pain, and a tear began to roll down his cheek. Another quickly followed, and he sobbed a few times to hold back from crying too much.

"I'm sorry, Oliver," Arthur said, rubbing his shoulder. "I know it's a big thing to find this out. But you've gotten old enough to know. And you'll still get presents."

"I really will?" he asked back.

"Yeah," Arthur laughed, which seemed to subdue Oliver's tears.

Mia walked into the kitchen, wearing a dark red blouse and tight black pants. She gave Arthur a look that seemed to ask if he approved, and he returned with eyes that said yes.

"You can go change now," she joked.

"I will, actually," he replied. "And I'll be fast. I'm starving."

"Good," she answered. "This is our fancy little Christmas dinner, and I'm starving too."

He kissed her on the cheek as he walked past, and the smell of her skin entered his senses. It was a part of her that hadn't changed. It was a scent so unique that he couldn't find a way to describe it, other than by her name, Mia.

"By the way," he said stepping into the hallway, "Oliver knows about Santa Claus."

It All Becomes Real
Or, When Death Becomes Sincere

Tears fell from Faye's eyes as she watched a dying squirrel violently convulse across salt-stained pavement. Just a moment before, a truck had quickly driven by, hitting the small animal and sending it to its death. Blood splattered the concrete. The squirrel's arms thrashed about in sharp movements. Its back legs, in complete contrast to its violent front, flailed limply behind.

Faye saw it all happen from the steps of her grandparents' house. She was sitting there waiting on Jeanne, who was still talking inside. At first, she didn't recognize what had happened. She saw the truck drive past and heard a strange thud. It was followed by a painful, squealing cry, and the sound of it made Faye feel horribly sad. She stood where she was, watching the dying squirrel jerk uncontrollably across the street.

In the face of this agony she had an impulsive desire. She was told not to leave the porch, and she knew Jeanne wouldn't be much longer, but she had to see what was happening. It was as if the universe knew what she was looking for and gave it to her right then and there.

She was terrified of what she might see, but she had to see it nevertheless. Faye turned to look at the front door. She saw no one, but heard voices from inside the house. It was worth the risk, she thought, and kicked off from the steps.

She ran to the edge of the lawn and stopped. She had gathered up the courage to leave the porch, but she didn't dare come close to the street. Besides, from where she was she saw well enough what had happened. Tears began to fall uncontrollably from her eyes. She stood sobbing in her red winter jacket, staring at the end of a small life not much different from her own.

She knew this was death because it made her feel exactly as she imagined she would. If she could it put into words, which she couldn't, it would be absolute helplessness and heartbroken fear.

The squirrel stopped moving and fell along the curb of the street. It breathed in rapid spasms, while its insides seemed to be convulsing in pain against its short brown fur. Its paws twitched inward and then slowly released back, repeating the movement over and over again, slower each time until it stopped completely. The convulsions soon followed, as did its breathing.

Faye never stopped looking, not until she heard Jeanne's voice yelling from behind. She wanted to think about what she saw, she wanted to figure out just what dying was, but all she could do was cry. When words moved into her mind, trying to explain what she experienced, they were shoved away by the image of the dead squirrel lying in a thin smear of blood.

She took two steps towards Jeanne and stopped. She couldn't breath from the painful sobs that pulled air into her lungs but wouldn't let it out.

"Faye, you get over here now!" Jeanne shouted. "Get away from that road. I told you to wait on the porch." Faye looked up to Jeanne's eyes. "Oh, honey," Jeanne said in a softer tone, seeing the tears upon the small girl's face. "What's wrong?"

Faye pointed back to the lifeless squirrel behind her.

"Oh, dear," Jeanne sighed, noticing the dead animal. She grabbed Faye by the hand and led her away from the scene, back up to the porch and into the warmth of her grandparents' house.

"What's the matter?" Faye's grandma asked with a worried look upon her face.

"Dead squirrel," is all Jeanne said as she walked with Faye into the living room. They sat upon the couch and Jeanne hugged her tight. "What you saw was something bad," she said, brushing away the hair that clung to Faye's tears, "but it's a part of life, a part of nature."

"I know," Faye coughed out between sobs, unable to say more. She understood what she saw, though there was still much that she didn't comprehend.

"I'm calling your father, okay?" Jeanne asked with sad eyes.

Faye nodded yes, and Jeanne walked into the kitchen for her phone. The sunlight was shining through the curtains behind Faye, and it illuminated her grandma as she sat down beside her. The two sat silently upon the sofa, listening to Jeanne talking on her phone in the other room.

Faye's mind was wakening from the sadness that had taken over, and she was starting to grasp exactly what she had seen. It was what would someday happen to her and everyone she knew. It's what would become of every life that lived.

Tears again fell from her eyes.

And her sadness cried her thoughts back to sleep.

Not Giving A Damn
Or, Giving A Damn

Oliver read the news.

The world was falling apart.

As far as he could remember, though, it always had been. People were relentlessly doing awful things to each other, killing, stealing, raping, and abusing the world around. And it wasn't just to each other. They did it to the planet they lived on too. They ruined the world day by day, polluting and destroying it whenever they seemed to have the chance.

It wasn't that Oliver was unsympathetic, or that he was completely pessimistic about humanity. He wanted the world to be a better place. He cared for the people in every tragedy that occurred. He longed for a human race that cherished the earth and shared compassion for one another. In fact, he knew there were many people who did just that. But he also knew that his desires wouldn't change the way things worked. Everything eventually dies. Why should humankind, and the planet upon which it lived, be any different?

But then again, he thought, seeing the sad news of children dying somewhere far across the world, shouldn't he strive against that decay? Just because he was going to die someday didn't mean he gave up on living. So just because the human race was doomed, it didn't mean that everyone should give in to the global suicide around them. Maybe things could change for the better. Maybe humanity could find its way out of its own selfish problems and start living in a more peaceful way.

Oliver wondered, however, if peace was really the point of it all.

Maybe existence was supposed to be difficult.

Without struggle what was there?

Endless happiness?

Would that even be happiness?

Sure it would, he decided.

But is happiness the point of it all?

His thoughts were colliding into each other, crashing and splitting into more and more questions. It was too much for him to think about. He had only fifteen minutes before his break was over.

Oliver finished scrolling through the article he was half-reading online and clicked a link that led him to another. It was a piece about the government and how they pretty much watched everything that happened on the Internet. It wasn't alarming news to Oliver. He had always assumed the government saw everything online, and he therefore didn't put anything on the Internet that he felt was personal. He despised the idea of some governmental agency spying upon everyone, so his way of protest was to not use the medium that was being watched. This wasn't a big loss to him anyway. He didn't really enjoy the Internet. It was too constricting to his life, too distorting to reality, and too alluring to the selfish desires within him that he wished to control.

He did, however, believe the Internet had the potential to be used for good. And he conceded that in some ways it was being used so now. But for the most part it was a foolish wasteland. It was a place for people to stare at nothing, shop for things they didn't need, entertain themselves in unentertaining ways, and, of course, masturbate to videos of other naked humans. All in all it was just being used as another way for people to forget the real world, even though it did have the latent ability to connect everyone together in positive ways.

Oliver stood from the computer desk that sat in the break room of Ouro's, and he walked out back for a cigarette. He grabbed his winter coat, which hung beside the door, and put it on. He pushed the backdoor open and walked into the cold air. The sky was a bright, flat gray. The air was dry, and the ground was snowless, covered instead in a thin layer of dusty salt.

Oliver fiddled in his pocket for his cigarettes and lighter. He pulled them out, placed one in his lips, and lit up. He exhaled a hot cloud of smoke into the cold air. He always enjoyed smoking in the winter. In fact, he didn't really like smoking during the warmer months. He needed the cold around his body to balance the heat within his lungs. He longed for the massive exhalation of smoke and moisture that left him in a cloud of white. Best of all was a clear winter sky, blazing into a crisp sunset as he smoked his thoughts away into the cold atmosphere around him.

Oliver's mind went back to the news he was reading. He compared it to the world he was in. The two nearly seemed to be opposites. Here he was, in an existence that was nothing other than itself. And in the other world, the place of words, everything was something else. Things didn't just exist as they were. There was a deeper meaning behind the cause and effect of it all. There was right and wrong and true and false. But in the life Oliver saw before him, the one in which he lived every day of his life, there was no deeper meaning to be found. There was only everything just as it was.

Through all the bad news that humanity could muster, this enduring universe would continue. So what was Oliver to do?

Take a stand against the decay?

Or gracefully die along with the world?

He took one last drag from his cigarette before snubbing it out and tossing it into a dirty plastic bucket beside the door.

He would have to think about life some other time.

For now, it was back to work.

Corporeal Movements
Or, Your Finite Potential

Her grandmother's veins pushed blue against the waxy wrinkled skin of the back of her hands. Claire felt a little unease while staring at them. It wasn't her grandma's hands themselves that disgusted her. It was the reminder they gave that did. They looked so alive, which thus meant they looked so possible of dying. What she stared at wasn't the simple concept in her head of the word hands. What she saw was the existent flesh and blood that made up her grandmother, the cells and tissues and organs that made up the mortal life of a human body. Claire knew she was made of the same stuff, and she feared the day that her hands would look so old, so real, and so close to death.

"I hope your sister will be all right," her grandmother said, pulling a thin, clear sheet of plastic wrap over a plate of peppermint brownies. She had made them for Faye, and Claire stopped by on her way home to pick them up.

"I'm sure she will be," Claire replied, still watching her grandma's hands. They moved with a slight shakiness as they tugged at the plastic wrap and folded it around the plate.

"Well, at least she has these," she said, handing the plate to Claire.

"Death is hard to understand when you're young," she said to her grandma, "but everyone has to do it. I know that firsthand."

At this, Claire's grandmother seemed to show the slightest grimace, which quickly disappeared into a look of sympathy. The two of them stood quiet, and Claire, for a brief moment, thought about the day she lost her mother. She saw her father holding back his tears, telling her that her mother was gone. She remembered sitting on the floor as he held her. She cried, at first with her face pressed into the carpet, but soon after into his shirt until it was sopping wet. She couldn't imagine the pain that he felt, not only when he found out his wife had died, but also in having to tell his children.

"She'll be okay," Claire reassured her grandmother. "I'll make sure. And so will Dad and Jeanne and Oliver."

"Mhmm," is all her grandma replied, lightly nodding her head.

"Well, I'd better go," Claire said, moving to her grandmother and hugging her with one arm.

"Take care of yourself, now," her grandma said, patting her hand gently on Claire's back.

"I will," she replied, turning to walk for the door. "Love you. And tell Grandpa I said the same."

She nodded, and Claire walked out of the kitchen. She walked to the door and opened it, feeling the cold air rush inward through the warm front room. She stepped out, took the small key ring out of her purse, and locked the door behind her.

The sun had disappeared. Its distant influence was all that remained, immersing the world in a heavy, dark blue. The air was cold and dry against Claire's skin. The muscles in her jaw quivered as she walked home. She felt the warmth of the plate against the palm of her right hand and wondered how her little sister was doing.

What did her young mind think about death?

About life?

About anything at all?

Thoughts

Or, Time

She was afraid of being awake so late at night.

She had never been up at such a mysterious time.

It wasn't that she wanted to. She longed to fall back asleep more than anything, yet she couldn't no matter how hard she tried. In fact, she was terrified she would never sleep again.

It was 3:00 a.m., and she felt like she was in a different world.

She had fallen asleep in her dad's arms. She cried to him about seeing the dead squirrel. She told him she was afraid of dying and that she was afraid of him and everyone else dying too. He told her that he wasn't going to die anytime soon and neither was she. He explained that dying was difficult, but even so it wasn't something you could ignore. It was a part of life, and we had to accept it and live on. The important thing, he told her, was to see the good in life.

The last thing she remembered, after talking to her dad, was eating peppermint brownies while curling up against his lap. Then she was here, in her bed at two in the morning. She had been lying in the dark and trying to sleep for the last hour, though her thoughts made it impossible.

What does it feel like to die?

What does it feel like to not exist at all?

That's what terrified her. She was afraid of not existing. It was an idea that seemed so strange. How could she not exist?

Sharp waves of realization would come to her when her childish contemplations of death would drift into an awareness of what it was that she knew. Someday she would die. Some second of her life would be the last, and everything she was would end. She felt this down to her bones, and it frightened her deeply. But soon the understanding would wane back into smaller thoughts, and her terror would subside.

Over and over again this happened, and eventually her small bedside clock, which lit up in bright red numbers, displayed 4:00 a.m.

She slid out of bed, switched on the little yellow lamp beside her dresser, and grabbed her book on death. It wasn't the one she chose from the library. It was the one that strangely showed up amongst her books. She again looked at its cover, which had a sad child holding the hand of an adult who could only be seen from the waist down.

"Where life goes," Faye whispered to herself, reading the title as she climbed back into bed. She opened the wide, thin book to its first page. Upon it was the boy from the front cover, but in this picture he looked happy. Beside him was an older person, perhaps his grandpa. He too was taller than the book, and Faye only knew he was old by the clothes that he wore. The small boy was running beside his grandpa and pointing at something in the distance. On the opposite page were words, which Faye read aloud. "I love my grandpa. We have fun together, going places and doing things. He is special to me, and he says I am special to him too."

She slowly turned the page, and in the silent room, the sound of paper moving against paper cut loudly through the stillness. Now there was a picture of the boy sitting on someone's lap. He was looking up into their eyes.

"Something happened though," she continued to read. "My parents told me I won't be able to see Grandpa anymore. They told me he had passed away. I didn't understand."

Faye understood completely, both what had happened to the kid's grandpa and how the kid was feeling. She was excited to turn to the next page, though her eyes were beginning to feel heavy.

The boy was looking down and standing alone as tears fell down his face. Behind him were trees colored orange and yellow and red.

"My grandpa died," Faye spoke softly. "My parents said that dying was a part of life, though life lasts a long, long time before most people pass away. Grandpa had lived a long, long time."

She turned the page of her book, where she saw the boy sitting beside some toys. Coming from the top of his head was a bubbly cloud, which meant the boy was thinking. Inside the cloud were images of the boy playing with his grandpa.

"We should be thankful for life," she read, her voice becoming slow. "We should remember the good times we had with people who have passed away."

She closed her eyes and turned the page. After a moment of stillness, she jerked awake and strained to see. There was another picture of the boy. He was crying yet again.

"But still," Faye read in a nearly silent whisper, "I feel sad when I think of Grandpa. I feel scared when I think of dying."

And her heavy eyes fell fast asleep, her book lying opened wide across her blankets and her little yellow lamp shining dim light throughout her room.

December 24th, 2006
Or, A Heavy Hollow Chest

Mia is dead.

He told this to himself everyday.

And everyday it sounded like the same damn lie.

How could she be dead?

She was everything.

How can everything die?

Every morning he would wake up to find her beside him, in the same place he found her every night as they fell asleep. She knew him more than any other person ever has or ever could. She was woven into his existence, and he into hers. Together they carved a path through life.

Mia had given birth to their children, creating existence from the depths of her body in the form of three beautiful human beings. He and his wife raised them with every fragment of love within their souls.

She was beautiful.

She was compassionate.

She was Arthur's love and Arthur's life.

And now she didn't exist.

He hadn't realized how alone he was without her. She made this hollow world a richer place, full of love and meaning and peace. Now that she was gone, he was drifting through a lingering emptiness.

A tear fell on Faye's cheek and ran slowly down her soft skin. She gently flinched and curled her arms inward. It wasn't her own liquid sorrow that slid across her face. It was her father's.

Arthur held his ten-month-old daughter in his arms and wept. In front of him was so much love, yet inside he felt desolate. With effort he pushed that sadness away, not into a place separate from himself, but a place hidden far within. He had to ignore his sorrow. His children needed him. Oliver was a teenager, which Arthur remembered being awkwardly difficult in every aspect. And even though it was a time for Oliver to grow away from home, it would be a much darker life to face without a mother's love to fall back on.

Claire was eleven years old. She still possessed the soft soul of a child, but she was beginning her transformation into another stage of life. She was growing into a teenager, entering into the same world that his son was living now. She needed the feminine guidance of her mother, but all she had was a sad and lonely father.

The two of them, Oliver and Claire, handled their mother's death quite differently, and in ways that were opposite of how Arthur thought they would. Oliver, who mostly kept to himself, was open about the immense sadness he felt. He trembled when Arthur first told him what had happened. It was as if his body wasn't able to handle the news. Shortly thereafter, when his sorrow finally took hold, Oliver painfully cried and gasped in empty breaths. For quite a while afterwards he openly talked about how he loved Mia, his mother, and how much it hurt to live without her.

Claire, on the other hand, was distant, even though she was honest and unreserved in all other aspects of her life. She cried when Arthur first told her, but afterwards her tears seemed to weep inward, hiding inside her head and not daring to come out. Arthur glimpsed her crying alone once, though he didn't let her know he did. She was standing in the kitchen, holding a glass of juice as tears fell down her face. He often tried to come to her, to get her to talk about her sadness, but she insisted she didn't have anything to say, that she was sad and that was that.

Then there was Faye. Born only this year, she would never know her mother. It was a wonder that she was born at all. Mia handled the pregnancy impossibly well. They hadn't planned on having another child, and they didn't think it would be likely anyway, so they went without the precautions. On a rainy day in mid-July, Mia told him the news. She was forty-one, he was forty-four, and they were having a baby. The next year, in February, they had their beautiful daughter, Faye. And three months later, Mia died.

She was driving across town to pick up some paint, which they were going to use in Faye's bedroom. A car, driven by a young woman of twenty-three, who also died, slammed into her side as she drove through an intersection. Mia's neck broke instantly, and her lungs collapsed. She was dead by the time the ambulance arrived. She died on her way to pick up two gallons of lavender paint. Her life ended for paint, and Arthur couldn't stop thinking that over and over again the day that it happened.

It was a painful year for him and his family. He had just published a book, a novel about a young man who lucid dreams his way into another life. It had yet to make much, if any, money. With only one parent in a house with three children, things began to become disordered. Oliver was old enough to help quite a bit, but there was no one who could come close to filling the gap that was left behind from losing Mia. Arthur's parents often came by, and his mother helped him raise Faye. If he had places to be or work to be done, she would watch his children for as long as he needed.

It was Christmas Eve, and Arthur stood in the living room of his parents' house, holding his daughter in his arms and fighting the sorrow in his head. Outside, the world was covered in a thin layer of snow, and the sky shone an empty, bright gray. His life felt like it had disappeared since the day that Mia died. The only importance left, the thin husk of meaning that shaped his otherwise empty existence, was the love he had for his children. It was they that gave him the frail strength he had left. And he knew that only through them could he find his way through this sadness.

The impermanence of everything, however, would often be too much. Not even his children could keep it away all the time. He lost his wife, and he knew that he could lose them too. This struck a deep terror within him, and many nights he would lie awake in fear that the next day would bring death.

Humans die.

His wife was a human.

His children were humans.

He was human.

"Dad," he heard Oliver say from the room behind. He turned to see his son standing tall, his long dark hair hanging across his face. "We're gonna play cards. You wanna join?"

"Sure," he said back with a faint smile.

Just then the sound of Christmas music came from across the house. It was the same Bing Crosby song he heard so long ago, when he sat in the backseat of his parents' car, understanding what it meant to love.

A Weighty Context
Or, Life's Floating Landscape

It was warmer than it had been, strangely so for a mid-December day, and Oliver felt the need to escape society for a while. He needed nature, untouched by man, and what it gave to him, which was a view into the reality hidden deep in plain sight.

On the edge of Moyenne was a forested park, not very large, but not very small either. Its rough trails meandered about large hills and deep hollows, being one of the few places around that had much change in elevation. This was probably the reason, Oliver thought, that it hadn't been developed into land for houses or schools or malls or offices. People disguised their inability to develop it with the virtuous claim that it should be a nature park.

As a teenager, Oliver spent many of his days there. It was a place for him and his friends to escape. They would sit in the woods, mostly wasting time doing nothing at all. It was even where he had his first kiss, which instilled into it a strange sense of being someplace sacred. It wasn't that the kiss was significant to him, or the girl, but rather the moment in which it took place. The two of them sat alone together, young and afraid and awakening to a new world. He leaned closer to her and looked into her eyes. As she looked back at him, the universe seemed to pull his lips forward. And the instant they kissed, Oliver became someone else.

Though who that was he hadn't yet found out.

The wind blew through the trees above, and the creaking of their wood resounded around Oliver. He walked along a path he had traveled before, though it had been many years since. The dirt beneath his feet was wet from the recently melted snow. The sky was a bright cold blue, though across it the sun shone warmly. The moist bark on the trees was nearly black, and the leafless branches above made wild, dark shapes against the sky.

More than all of this, Oliver sensed the smell of the damp woods surrounding him. It was the scent of warmth meeting the cold, briefly awakening nature from its early winter sleep. He could smell the earth below as the meltwater crept into its dry, frozen crevices and aroused a musty odor. The muskiness, much like the smell after a summer rain, though in a colder, sharper way, began to fade into the smell of the pines that appeared along the path. Their bittersweet scent overtook Oliver's emotions and pushed him into a deeper sense of being. Nature always had the ability to awaken within him a real connection to life, and, at the same time, death. It was a uniting of his self with what really existed, and it was within that reality that he looked for answers.

But even though he felt that sacred truth swim about the smells in his nose, the lights in his eyes, and the sounds in his ears, he didn't feel it within his mind. Instead, inside of him were endless, crowded, shallow thoughts. And those very thoughts were what he knew to be Oliver, the person he was in his normal life. It was a weight upon his shoulders simply being that self, a product of a generation obsessed with fun. His brain was shaped by entertainment, by the nineties, by TV and video games and words and people. He was an imaginary life in an imaginary world, looking through a peephole into a reality so far away.

He was searching for truth, though deep down he knew that what he sought didn't exist. It was a fantasy within him and nothing more. The only thing that actually existed was what was already there.

Nature.

But there was where he was, and there he couldn't see a thing. It wasn't until he gave up looking that he found the truth, which was emptiness. When he stopped asking loud questions, the silent answers came to him. But he didn't see the truth or hear the answers, because they were none other than the absence of themselves. And so he never realized that he had found what he was looking for, as he walked alone, dreaming of the place that he was already in.

Forwards
Or, Backwards

Claire gazed out of the car window. Houses that she had seen pass by countless times before passed by yet again. She turned to her father, who sat to her left. He was driving with a serious look on his face, one that Claire knew well. It meant he was thinking of what to say and soon he would say it.

"You know," he said, "life is pretty funny sometimes. Or, all the time, really." He seemed to be directing his words at Faye, who sat in the backseat, though as he spoke he glanced to Claire. "It can be good, and then bad, and then good again. The important thing is to keep your head up and just live."

"And to love people too, right?" Faye asked.

"And to love people too," he replied, nodding his head. "That's what living is after all. Loving people and the earth and everything there is."

Claire shifted in her seat and rested her head upon the window. She knew that what her father said was simply a way to cheer up Faye. There may have been some truth to it, but it was mostly kitsch sentimentality. Real life is deeper than that. It's about more than love and happiness and being good. What exactly it was about, Claire didn't know, but she knew that it wasn't that.

The car came to a stop at an intersection. Faye hummed a song to herself in the back. It sounded familiar to Claire, but it wouldn't come to her mind.

"So how about we get a movie at the library?" her father asked. "We should get something Christmasy. *Rudolf* or *Frosty* or something."

"Sure," Claire replied.

Faye stopped humming her song.

"Whatcha think, Faye?" he asked her, looking into the rearview mirror.

"Okay," she said back, as if her thoughts were somewhere else. Claire watched her father's face gently sadden as he returned his eyes to the road.

She wondered what went on in Faye's head, and then realized it was probably the same stuff that went on in hers when she was seven years old. Everything was something. The littlest moments, ideas, and feelings became the center of the universe. Life was simpler, yet at the same time it was possible of so much joy and terror that there was never any rest.

Claire wondered what had changed in her life from then to now. What made her become who she was? Was it her own doing? Or was she simply the effect of all the causes that led up to now? One thing came to Claire's mind more than anything else—the death of her mother. Something changed within her then. She became a little darker, a little more skeptical of the world. She kept up the façade of being who she was, a naïve little girl, but from then on she knew that she was different inside. And now the years of hiding that transformation had finally caught up to her. She couldn't stand being Claire anymore.

Though she wasn't sure she could stand being anyone at all.

She wrapped her hand around the bracelet on her wrist and felt the mantra adorned upon it with her fingers. What could she do to find herself? What would make her happy?

Her father pulled the car into the library parking lot.

"We're here," he said, lightly smiling.

"Let's get *Frosty the Snowman*," Faye suddenly said, and to this his smile widened.

Claire opened the door of the car and turned, setting her feet down onto the wet pavement outside. She gave a heavy sigh and stood, thinking of her mother and what she would have done.

She remembered a moment from long ago when she was eight. Her mother had taken her to the art museum. It was just the two of them together, walking along the dimly lit hallways, staring at the paintings and talking about what they meant.

"Just imagine all these people," her mother said, "living their own lives and thinking their own thoughts. So much creativity. So much difference." Her mother looked to her, and she could still remember well the look in her eyes as she asked, "How do you want to live your life, Claire?"

But she couldn't remember the answer.

Or if she even had one.

December 24th, 2009
Or, Softness

Arthur opened his eyes to the morning light shining through his bedroom windows. He had no hopes of going back to sleep, thanks to the bright white glow that overtook the room and the rambling thoughts in his head that seemed to awaken before he did.

It was Christmas Eve, and he imagined the day ahead.

He would first spend time with his daughters. He would make them breakfast, and they would sit around in their pajamas eating and talking and laughing. His son would later come over and spend the rest of the day with them, and in the evening they would go to the family Christmas party. He would have to make awkward small talk with distant relatives, but he would nonetheless enjoy being around them. They were his family, and every day that meant something more.

Finally, late at night, he would have to stay up and play Santa, leaving presents beneath the plastic Christmas tree in the living room.

He missed Mia.

The thought often broke into his mind out of nowhere, especially in the mornings, when he would lie alone in bed. The sharp pain of losing her had been eroded into a dull ache, but in its softness it grew wide across his life. Now his days were strewn with delicate moments of sadness, and as the moments passed by they would leave empty spaces inside of him. It was then that he pushed inward with all the strength he had, filling the hollows within himself with life. He was resilient against his misery. Being a father was more important to him than any emotions that stirred within his painful head and heart. But for himself he also fought his depression, which was a difficult thing to do. He didn't want to be happy. He didn't want to face life with hopefulness. His love had been taken away, and it wouldn't be right for him to continue on as if it had never happened. But as time went by he realized the truth of his situation. He accepted that she was gone, that he would have to let go of his sadness, and that he would inevitably feel happy again.

"Dad?" a quiet voice said beside him. It was Faye.

Arthur rolled onto his side to see her climbing into his bed. She gave a small grunt as she pulled herself up over the edge, pressing her face into his blankets.

"Dad?" she asked again, muffled beneath the covers.

"Yes, Faye," he replied. She crawled across the bed until her face was inches from his.

"Santa comes tomorrow morning?" she asked. He nodded yes. "So he doesn't come this morning?" she continued.

"Nope," he replied, rubbing his eyes.

"Oh, okay," she said, pressing her hands against his chest. He smiled and wrapped his arms around her.

"But it is Christmas Eve," he told her, "and we've got lots of fun things to do."

"Like what?" she asked, squirming away and staring at him with her hazel eyes.

"Well, we get to spend time with each other. It's nice to have a whole day with your family."

"Yeah, it is," she said, rolling onto her back. "What are we gonna do together?"

"We can make pancakes for breakfast," he said, sitting up. "And we can play some games or watch a movie. We can do whatever we want. And tonight we'll go to the Christmas party. And then it's to bed before Santa gets here."

"Do you think I'll get somethin' good?" she asked.

"It depends. Have you been good?"

"Well, I've been okay," she answered, sitting up and brushing the hair away from her face. "So I bet I get okay stuff."

"I'm sure you'll get good presents," he told her.

"What about Claire?" she asked.

"I think she's been good," he said. "Don't you?"

"Yeah. She's been okay too. What about Oliver?"

"Well, he's been alright. But Santa doesn't visit him anymore."

"Why?" she asked.

"He's gotten too old. Santa doesn't get me any presents either, does he?"

"No, I guess not. When will I be too old?"

"Oh, it's hard to say. It's different for everyone."

"Can we watch a movie?" she asked, suddenly changing the subject.

"What about breakfast?" Arthur replied, getting out of bed.

"I'm not hungry," Faye said, jumping off the bed and running to the doorway.

"Yes, you are," he told her.

"Nope," she replied, shaking her head.

"Yes, you are," he said again.

"Just a little bit," she gave in.

"Well, c'mon," he said, picking her up. "Let's go start today."

You Are What You Are
Or, You're Not You At All

"So is Frosty the hat, or is he the snowman?" her father asked.

"What?" Faye replied, not understanding the question.

"Frosty came to life when the hat got put on the snowman. So is he the hat or is he the snowman?"

"Uhm, the hat!" she answered.

"The snowman!" Jessica shouted.

"I think he's both," her father said a moment later, after setting a bowl of popcorn onto the table. "The snowman isn't Frosty without his hat, but the hat isn't Frosty without the snowman."

"I don't think the girls are in a philosophical mood, Arthur," Jeanne said, walking into the room.

"We should watch something else," Jessica proclaimed, grabbing a handful of popcorn and shoving it into her mouth. She dropped a few of them, but didn't notice.

Jessica had come over to spend the night with Faye, which Arthur had suggested at the library when they were checking out. After they got home, Faye called to see if her friend could stay the night. Her parents said she could, and a few hours later the two girls were watching Christmas movies and laughing.

Faye was glad her friend was there. She didn't want to think about what she had been thinking about lately. Yet, even though she was having fun, she was tired from barely sleeping last night.

Her dad walked by and stood beside the television.

"How about *A Christmas Carol*?" he asked.

"The one with Kermit the Frog?" Jessica asked back.

"Mhmm," he replied, nodding.

"Sure!" Faye said, taking some popcorn from the bowl. She ate them one by one as her father started the movie. After it began he walked out of the room with Jeanne. Before they left, however, Faye heard Jeanne whisper into her father's ear. He replied with a smile and a slow wave of his hand.

The two girls now sat alone, watching the movie and eating popcorn. Faye's attention slowly faded, even though she liked the movie. Her eyes grew heavy as she stared at the television.

"Who's your favorite Muppet?" Jessica asked.

"I dunno," Faye replied, turning to her friend, who continued to stare at the television.

"Mine's Kermit," she said, grinning at the screen.

"I like Kermit too," Faye replied, "But I think, maybe, I like Gonzo the most."

"Gonzo? He's weird."

"Yeah, that's why I like him."

"I hate Miss Piggy. She's annoying. Poor Kermit."

"Yeah, she is. But she's okay. She's nice sometimes."

Jessica said nothing else, and Faye returned to the television screen. Her eyes again grew heavy, so much so that they were closed more than they were open. She fell asleep a few times, just for quick moments, nodding awake and catching a glimpse of the movie.

She finally fell and remained asleep just as Scrooge met the Ghost of Christmas Yet To Come. She thought it was a dream, half awake and half asleep. The hooded man without a face, who both terrified and excited her, took her into darkness, where she slept as well as the dead.

Alone
Or, Alone

Oliver's lips were stained a muddy violet from cheap merlot. He was standing in the dim golden light of his living room, searching with heavy eyes a row of paintings that leaned against the wall. He was hoping to find something beautiful.

After all, his art was everything he had.

He kneeled beside a tall canvas painting, caressing his hand against its thick acrylic paint. His eyes followed the dense black line that traced an indistinct, yet alluringly suggestive, form. Quick, sharp cuts of black paint bled into soft curves that overlapped upon themselves in smooth organic movements. Behind the meaningless figure were splashes of deep cyan and vibrant yellow. Every fraction of the painting was beautiful to him, but he knew that no one else would think the same. It was only his ego relishing in what it had done. He could have seen beauty in any piece of trash that he made.

He stood back from the painting and took the last drink from his glass of wine. He thought of what to do with himself. His life was going nowhere. But in truth, did he really even want it to go somewhere? Was happiness, to him, a gentle no thank you to life?

Was drifting through his existence all that he really wanted?

Why do anything at all?

Because he needed that hidden something that he saw missing from himself. He wasn't even sure what it was, but he knew he desired it more than anything. Maybe it didn't even exist. Maybe it was just a dream inside his dreams. Forever he would be in search of something unattainable.

Michelle was right.

He believed in nothing.

And that nothing was what he lived for.

"Shit," he said to himself, because the universe needed to say and hear it. He walked to his bedroom and opened his closet doors. Pushing aside a bundle of old T-shirts he didn't wear anymore, he pulled out the *Little Nemo* box that held his stash. Sitting cross-legged on the floor, he ground up a large bud and packed a bowl in his green glass pipe, enjoying the smell that came to him all the while.

Oliver wasn't drunk from the wine, but his thoughts were loosened and free from his normal constraints. It was at this stage of intoxication that he usually felt the best, but it was also when he couldn't resist the urge to go for more. He craved being lost in an altered state of mind, which endlessly led him onward into strange influences, be they chemical, physical, mental, or emotional. He wanted nothing other than to escape the average experience of his life, even if it meant leaving himself behind.

He burned a bowl alone, listening to the foreign electronic music that played from his stereo. Gazing at the string of Christmas lights he had hung across his bedroom window, he filled his lungs with the potent smoke of his pipe. After a few heavy hits, followed by a few heavy coughs, the world became dreamlike, yet at the same time Oliver's mind and body became more real. Bizarre thoughts came to him from a place far within, and he questioned his life in every way possible. He doubted the human organism that made up who he was, letting anxiety flood in and conquer his mind. His body existed far too much. His muscles quivered and his spine ached. He was a thin, delicate presence sitting close to death.

It was then that he truly believed he was dying.

But Oliver didn't die.

He wouldn't for quite some time.

Instead, he only sat scared and alone, facing all the endless possibilities that could come to him. Anything could happen, no matter how crazy it seemed. The entire universe was judging him and his life, which in reality was just his own mind judging itself. To him, however, he was in the hands of vengeful chaos.

Oliver forced himself to calm down. He knew the way his head worked, and he was familiar with the anxieties that came about when he was high. They were the same fears he had in normal life, only amplified through a lens of radical awareness. His high anxiety melded into his normal mindset, and the two met in a strange place somewhere between paranoia and insight. He knew that anything was possible, that his existence, which was very much a mortal one, was just a small part of an infinite universe of infinite potentials, and he nearly believed that something ridiculous would happen to him right then and there.

But more sensibly, and heavily, he acknowledged that he was simply alive. That meant he would have to someday die, and that someday could always be today.

Oliver stood up and stumbled to the tall black bookshelf in the corner of his room. He gazed at the many books that lined its shelves, losing himself in contemplation of what he was searching for. After a minute of mumbling some of the names of the books, he both remembered and found what he sought. He pulled a small, black volume from the shelf and fell onto his nearby bed. There, he opened up the book, which was a thin introduction to Eastern philosophy and religion. As he did so, a colorful drawing of a man in a red cap fell out. He picked the picture up, holding it in his hands and squinting his eyes in confusion. The man had a wide, peaceful grin upon his face, and behind him was a sea of blue. Swimming in its depths were fish of every color, shape, and size.

"Jacques Cousteau!" Oliver shouted to himself, remembering the drawing he had done a few years back. It was made during his obsession with the sea, which resulted in nothing at all since he lived in the middle of America and lacked the ambition and courage to follow his dreams. Instead, he spent days fantasizing of the vast sea, with its endless extraordinary life and mysterious unknown depths. From his landlocked hometown he imagined the distant sublimity, while slowly his desire faded away.

The drawing chiseled at a veiled and hardened part of Oliver, and through the cracks in his mind a feeling that had long been forgotten emerged. It was a dreamful aspiration buried deep within. It wasn't yet free, yet its light broke though, enough so to shine upon his thoughts. It was then that his inspiration began to reawake.

Returning to his book, which he had sought in the hope that his current state of mind would be more conducive to understanding it, he stared at the page that was held by his drawing. It was the beginning of a chapter on Buddhism. On the left hand page was an illustration of the Buddha sitting with his piercing yet half closed gaze.

Oliver returned the stare with his bloodshot eyes and felt strangely as if he was looking at himself. He slowly began to read the first paragraphs of the chapter, which were full of information he already knew. Yet even though he was familiar with what he was reading, he understood and experienced it in a way he never had before. He saw the four noble truths within his life, right then and there. He felt the emptiness in all things, yet the possible fullness in their relations with each other.

But still he was not free from the confines of his melancholy. Maybe, he thought, he didn't really understand. He still had desires, and he was rather fond of them, really. His tastes in existence were what guided his life. Without his desires, who would he be? No one? Well, yes, he decided, that is who he would be. And wasn't that the point? Maybe he was just too weak to accept that? But didn't he believe in nothing? Why was it so hard for him to let go of what he didn't believe in? Why did he hold on to that which kept him in his state of despair?

His nervousness crept back as he felt his body returning to an anxious state. He turned the pages of his book in hopes of finding something to ease his mind. He found himself reading a section on Taoism. It explained the endless fluid oneness that was existence, and it described the proper way to live alongside, and within, that flowing universe. The passive wisdom it expressed relieved Oliver's anxiety, and his attention drifted away into a place detached from reality and pain. He rolled from his bed, dropping the book upon his table. As his feet reached the ground he stepped on the drawing of Jacques Cousteau.

"No!" Oliver yelled out, twisting around and pausing for a moment. He picked the picture up and tossed it aside, quickly forgetting what had even happened. He fell on the floor where he sat before and took a few more hits from his pipe. He was feeling calmer, he thought, so why not get higher? He wanted an escape, and that was what he would get.

After smoking for a moment, he stood and walked across the room. He lit some candles that sat on his dresser and then turned all of the lights off. He tripped over something he didn't recognize as he walked back to his bed. Once there, he lay staring at the dark room and quivering candlelight that played upon the ceiling. He listened to the slow ambient music that drifted from his stereo, and he floated away to somewhere far from his bedroom. His eyes were now closed and his mind was now open. There was an image within him that was taking over. It was there that he existed.

It was a place that had no meaning, and thus it had all the meaning that could ever be. It was blue and dark. Then it was red and bright. There was yellow. And there was orange. And then everything went black. There were people appearing, but they weren't human. They were bodies of glowing white amongst the dark landscape. They moved about as if they were busy, yet none of them seemed to be doing anything at all.

The world began to sway to a wind that wasn't there, and suddenly someone stood in the center of his vision. It was a woman. He could tell so from the soft curves of her body. She didn't glow like the others. Instead, her skin was matte white. Her eyes burned bright with all the colors Oliver could imagine. For a brief moment he felt that everything was perfect.

She held out her hand, and he opened his eyes, leaving her and the beautiful world within his head behind.

Oliver was stoned as hell. He gazed at his dark room, focusing on the cold glow of moonlight that cut through the blinds of his window. He closed his eyes again and tried to drift into another vision. He was fed up with reality and the boundaries it imposed. He wanted a fantasy that had no limitations, but the real world wouldn't let him go. His mind was rambling and the world around him was pulling at his attention. He rolled out of bed and switched on the light. After blowing out the candles, he took one more hit from his pipe and then left his bedroom.

He stumbled through his apartment and ended up back in front of his paintings. This time he saw something different. In the mingling of paint upon canvas, Oliver saw a meaning that was new to his eyes. It was the expression of the point where he and his world collided. It was both how he viewed life and how life viewed him. And in the splatters of color and lines he saw, within that sacred location where he and the outside world met, the truth of what he was.

He wasn't Oliver.

And he wasn't the world.

He was the romance between the two, the endless passion of the universe loving and hating itself.

He was, in other words, nothing at all.

But there wasn't any grandeur in the realization. No enlightenment came to him. Everything was still the same, and that's just the way it would be. What more of an answer could the universe give other than its own presence?

Oliver grabbed his pack of cigarettes from the kitchen table and stepped out onto the balcony. The moon was full above, and the world was aglow with a sapphire light. Distant streetlights burned contrastingly orange against the cold. The air met Oliver's breath in a cloud of thick vapor. As he pulled out the sole cigarette left in his pack, it bent against the cardboard and snapped apart. He held it in front of his eyes and stared at the dangling stick of tobacco, which fell to the balcony as a small wind gusted by.

"Whatever," Oliver said, gazing at the moon.

Cherry Cola
Or, An Instant Lifetime

Claire couldn't stop staring at the way his eyes smiled to match his lips. She had never seen anyone's face look so genuinely happy. At first she felt attracted to his blissful demeanor. She wanted to know more about this boy named Joel. What made him tick? How could someone be so pleased with life? But some jealous part of her thoughts decided she didn't like the way he carried himself. Maybe he was simply faking it. Not in the sense that he pretended to be happy, but rather he was so naïve that his happiness was superficial. Perhaps he knew of no dark side to life. Had he never experienced the pain of loss, or the pain of countless other sorrows? What a shallow happiness it would be, Claire thought, if it wasn't gained from truly understanding the whole of life.

"So, you're going where?" Megan asked him.

"South Carolina," he answered, smiling in his candid way. Claire wondered what made him so satisfied with the thoughts in his head. What was it that made such happiness reveal upon his lips?

"South Carolina?" Claire asked, hoping to find out more about him. "What's there?"

"My sister and her family," he replied, looking straight into her eyes. She couldn't handle his directness, so she pretended to be looking at something in the distance as he continued to talk. "I've got two twin nephews. They're just under three years old. I haven't seen them since they were born."

"Awww!" Madison cried before taking a drink from her soda. The group then sat silent for a moment, and the sound of the nearly empty fast food restaurant took over. A busy kitchen in the back made hectic noise as junk food was cooked for the drive-through customers who would still be coming for hours. A few tables away, two worn-out looking parents sat with their child, who looked to be eight or nine years old. The two of them silently ate their cheeseburgers while their son rambled on about something Claire couldn't understand.

"You know, Claire's a vegetarian too," Megan said suddenly to Joel. "Aren't you?" she asked, turning to Claire.

"Yeah," she replied, nodding and giving a half-smile.

"Oh, really?" he asked. "For how long?"

"My whole life," she answered. "My parents raised me that way. They were vegetarian themselves."

"Wow!" he said so genuinely that Claire couldn't help but to smile. "That's awesome. I've only been one for a couple years. But it's great. I feel so much better. And it's good for the Earth too, ya know?"

"Yeah," she replied, continuing to smile.

"I just couldn't do it," Megan said before eating a small handful of french fries.

"It's easy," Joel told her. "I don't even want meat anymore. It's kind of gross, really." He turned to Claire. "Don't you think?"

"Definitely," she answered. This time she kept her eyes on him, though he quickly turned away.

"What about you?" he asked, looking to Madison.

"Oh, I don't know. I don't really eat much meat anyway," she said. "Just chicken sometimes."

"Fifty-four!" a tired-looking Hispanic girl yelled from behind the counter. "Fifty-four!"

"Oh, that's me." Madison said, standing up and walking to the counter. Claire watched her as she did, criticizing what she wore, how she walked, and even what she believed went on in Madison's head. It was a projection of disgust for exactly the kind of person Claire wanted to escape in herself, which was a common, self-centered teenager.

"So, we're going to Justin's tonight?" Megan asked.

"Yeah," Joel replied. "He's having a few people over. Plus he's got a pretty nice house. Have you seen his living room?"

"Nope," Megan replied.

"Huge," Joel answered. "Watching his TV is like going to the movies. And he's got this big couch that wraps around two of the walls. And his parents are great. They're super nice and pretty much do their own thing when Justin's got people over. His dad makes a ton of money."

"Doing what?" Claire asked, just as Madison returned with her order of fries and a chicken sandwich.

"Business stuff," Joel replied. "Stocks or loans or something like that. But even for all that money I couldn't do it. I'd go crazy. I need something a little more hands-on. A little more real."

"Yeah," Claire agreed, nodding.

"I think I might go to school for carpentry when I graduate," he said, taking a drink from his cherry cola. "I've done some work with my uncle before. He's a contractor. I liked it all right. And at least I wouldn't be playing with numbers all day."

"Oh, god! I hate math," Megan added in.

"What about you, Claire?" he asked.

Hearing him speak her name made something stir curiously within her, and instantly she could only think about him.

"I'm not really sure," she said, getting slightly choked up.

"I understand," he replied. "There's so many things to do, but most of it seems boring."

"Yeah," she said, brushing her hair aside. "It does."

"I'm going for nursing," Madison said, unwrapping her sandwich. "There's a lot of demand for it."

"Gross," Megan said. "You'd have to deal with really sick and old and fat people."

"Yeah," Madison replied, "but at least I'll have a job."

"Hey, I'm going to be a teacher." Megan responded. "There's always gonna be kids, so we're always gonna need teachers."

Claire broke away, with much effort, from her mental infatuation with Joel, and she wondered what she would be doing five years from now. The startling realization that eventually it would be five years from now came to her in a heavy wave. She thought about five years ago and how time took so long to get here. But she was nonetheless here, and looking back it all seemed to happen in an instant. So wouldn't her inevitable future come about in the same way? Life would move slowly along until suddenly she would be ten, twenty, thirty years older. And looking back, all those years in between would seem like a mere second.

"Hey, we should go," Joel said, looking at his cell phone.

"I just started eating!" Madison shouted.

"We'll wait," Megan said, turning to Joel. "When she's done cramming her face, I'll drive us to Justin's. I know the way, I think." She glanced at Claire and flashed a quick smile. "Why don't you and Claire go ahead?"

At this, Claire's chest felt heavy, though not in a painful way. She knew that she felt something for Joel, but she wasn't sure what. Maybe it was simply a fascination for how he acted, a modest interest in a person she had never met before.

Or maybe she felt something more?

"Sure," Joel replied. "If Claire wants to."

"I'll go," she answered without thinking.

"Cool," Megan grinned, standing up so that Joel could slide out of the booth seat. Claire stood as well and put on her jacket.

"We'll see you guys soon, then," Joel said, standing beside the table. Claire gave a sharp look to Megan, and Megan returned it with the same eyes.

"Ready?" Joel asked.

"Yup," Claire answered, turning and walking to the glass doors with big cling-on pictures of fountain drinks on them. Joel reached them before her and pushed them wide open, letting her pass through first. "Thanks," she said quietly, turning her face away from the cold wind that rushed in. The two of them walked through the parking lot to Joel's little red Toyota.

"It's not fancy," he said, "but it gets me around." He unlocked the doors and the two of them got in. The pleather and plastic interior creaked as they shifted in their seats. Joel turned the ignition and the neon green dashboard came to life.

"Tonight should be fun," he said, turning his head and backing out of the parking spot.

"Yeah, it should," Claire replied, not really knowing if it would be or not. It might at least be a night to remember, she thought, when someday she'd look back in time at the slow yet instantaneous flow of life, wondering where it all went and where it all would go.

December 24ᵗʰ, 2012
Or, How The Universe Heals Itself

"My son died when he was fourteen," Jeanne said with invisible tears collecting in her eyes. Arthur could see they were there even though they were hidden well by her acceptance of what had happened. "He was with his dad. It was the middle of July. This wasn't long after John and I had split up, and Corey took it so well. He understood how we felt and why we couldn't be together." Her tears began to take shape, emerging from their veiled existence. She looked away from Arthur and gently fidgeted with the empty wineglass in her hands. "He was so mature for his age, really. You could just see it in his eyes. They always looked so sincere." She paused for a moment. "But to go on, he was with his dad. They were visiting John's parents for the weekend. Corey had brought along a couple of friends. There was this lake nearby with a big wooded area full of trails and such. They loved to hang out there.

"It was Saturday night, about 7 o'clock or so. The boys were riding their bikes along the trails. Corey was really into bicycles. He wanted to go mountain biking so bad, and this was as close as he could get, or rather, as close as I would let him get.

"So they were riding around the trails and whatnot, and Corey had gotten far ahead of the others. According to them, they heard a crash followed by a scream and then a strange sound they didn't recognize."

She wiped away the tears that had formed in her eyes and slid her empty glass across the table to Arthur. She sat quiet as he filled it with what wine was left in the bottle.

"They couldn't find him, at least not at first. They rode back and forth on the trail, and then one of them saw his bike a little down the hill beside them. They ran to it, but he wasn't there. What they did find was a large rock smeared with blood. That's when they started yelling out his name. One of them went back to the house to get help, while the other searched down the hill. Scott Euler, the poor kid. He was the one that found him." She took a drink of wine and stared heavily at the air in front of her. "Corey had fallen and hit his head, which knocked him unconscious. That's why he drowned when he fell into the lake. The kid that found him said Corey was floating face down, and that the water was red all around the top of his body. He said he ran into the lake and flipped him over, but when he saw Corey's pale face he didn't know what to do. By the time John got there it was too late."

Arthur felt the need to speak, but he first let silence reply to her painful story. Jeanne stared down into her glass of red wine, while he gazed at the nearby Christmas tree and thought of what to say. His own children came to mind. He pictured Faye sleeping upstairs in her bed, dreaming of the Christmas morning that would soon come. And he thought of Claire and Oliver, growing through some of the most exciting times of life. He imagined losing them, which was a thought that had often haunted his past. The woman beside him had gone through just that. She had lost her child. She had lost herself.

"I'm so sorry," he said quietly, unsure if he should have said it at all. It was, of course, the considerate thing to say, but he knew she had heard it time and time again.

"That was eight years ago," she said, looking to him, "and I've accepted what's happened. But every day I still think of him, and for a moment I feel exactly as I did the day he died."

"I understand," Arthur told her. "Well, maybe not exactly. But I do understand. I know what it's like to lose someone close. I imagine nothing compares to losing a child though."

"The feeling," she said, choking on her words. "It's like your insides are on fire, yet your body doesn't even exist. All that you are is the sorrow. I'll see his smile and his eyes. I'll hear the words that he spoke. And the most painful of all is when I think of the life he would have lived."

"You said you accepted it. How?" Arthur asked, wanting to know more about her, as well as needing to connect with someone who shared the experience of death.

"It took a lot of time," she told him, pausing to drink the last bit of wine in her glass. "That's for sure. But it was mostly stepping back from my life that let me see what really happened. Death is all around us. Life is death, really, and when you see yourself and the ones you love as a part of the whole you can start to accept it. The hardest part of that is stepping away from yourself, because the people you love are a part of you, and that means stepping away from them as well."

"The hardest part for me wasn't stepping back from it all," Arthur replied, wrapping both of his hands around his glass. "I was already pretty far away from life. Too far, actually. For me, it was being able to experience life up close that was tough. I had always believed in the..." He paused to think of the right word to say. "...impermanence of everything. I could acknowledge that everyone dies, including those closest. What I couldn't handle was what remained after the fact. I had accepted the end, but not the beginning that followed."

"Hmm," Jeanne replied.

Arthur couldn't tell what she meant by it. Did she understand? Or did it mean the opposite? Was it an empathetic hum or a sign of confusion? He quickly pushed his thoughts away and ridiculed himself for thinking too much.

"I could let go," he continued on, "but I couldn't hold on. The sadness got less and less every day, but nothing took its place. It was if I had died too." He looked to Jeanne, who sat beside him with an expression of empathy. "How could I feel happy? Or feel anything at all? Someone close to me was gone, and yet there I remained. What right did I have to be whole while a part of me was missing?"

"How did you handle that?" she asked with a certain look in her eyes. Arthur could feel the difference in their losses. Hers was the death of a child. His was a lover. And the fact that Jeanne was, in truth, a replacement for that loss weighed heavy upon the conversation.

"Well, I guess I forced myself at first," he said, rubbing his hand through his thick, graying hair. "Mostly for Faye and Claire and Oliver. They needed me. And as I started living again, even though it was forced, I began to move closer to life. Almost the opposite of what you did, I suppose. And as I got nearer, I found a compassion deep within. It was for myself." He paused, unsure of what he was about to say. "And it was for Mia."

He looked into Jeanne's eyes, searching for a reaction. There was one, but he couldn't untangle it from the distance between them. He didn't yet know the woman in front of him. They had only met two months ago, when she had started working at the community college he taught at. She was hired on as the manager of the small bookstore that sold mostly school supplies, junk food, and textbooks. They had started talking every day as he passed by on his way to class. Their conversations grew in length and depth, and their words were touched with a subtle tenderness. Over the course of a week, Arthur realized he was attracted to her. It was a strange feeling for him. He hadn't experienced it since Mia. And as he asked Jeanne out for dinner, which took a tremendous amount of courage, he felt a lingering sense of guilt within his thoughts. That night, as he lay alone in bed, he spoke to Mia in whispers, telling her he had found someone whom he could possibly love. He cried, apologizing to her for moving on, and then he calmed himself in reassurance that what he was doing was right. Before he fell asleep, he spoke to Mia one last time. He told her that he still missed her and that he always would.

"I understand your compassion for yourself, but why for Mia? I thought you had already accepted her death?" Jeanne asked.

"I had accepted it," he told her, "but I was still holding on to what was left. I found that out when I got closer to myself. I was being selfish, keeping her life for my own. So I learned to let myself live, and I learned to let her die."

"So," Jeanne said after a still and silent moment, hesitating as she seemed to think deeply about what she was about to say, "you've really moved on?"

"I have," Arthur replied, staring at Jeanne through the warm lights of his candle lit living room. Her eyes showed sympathy, while her lips gave an affectionate smile. It was an expression that spoke to Arthur, letting him know her acceptance of who he was and her desire to become a part of his life, not as a replacement for what he had lost, but rather as a fully new piece that could mend his heart.

His eyes spoke to her as well, conveying his desire for everything that she was. He wanted to move closer to her, but he felt the time wasn't right. This wasn't about their bodies, but rather their hearts and minds. They caressed each other's inner scars and embraced the wholeness of who they were. They spoke through the night, as the snow fell heavy and cold outside.

Slowly, however, as the conversation of their souls grew close and still, their bodies stole away the night and found the touch of a new lover's skin.

Always Ending
Or, Never Beginning

For a time unknown he didn't exist.

Then, uplifted from the void, he did.

Being the child of nothingness, he experienced an immensity too grand for him to understand. There was no self to hinder the unbounded creativity that flowed into the emptiness. There was only awareness, so pure in its existence that it was nothing other than that which it perceived.

A primordial emotion, absolute in its sincerity, danced forth from this egoless point. It was love and hate and fear and ecstasy all joined together into one sensation.

Within that first sentiment a nebulous passage was formed. It traveled from nowhere to somewhere through a strange new connection with a mind that was about to be born.

In full speed, Oliver's life spread wide its wings of perception and flew through the vague corridor of his dreams. Every aspect of this inner world became an echo of his ordinary mind. The people and places of his waking life came forth in mirrored ways. The awareness from before, which then was so pure and light, was now tainted with a heavy dread that drifted from his normal way of thinking. The sincere and faceless emotion that once gushed forth had now taken on the disenchanted nuances of Oliver's ego.

However, there was still a certain deepness to the world that his persona couldn't push away. He was standing so close to the beginning, the end, and the middle of it all. There he was where he was born, where he would live, and where he would die. Sacredness pulsed all around him, and it merged with his dream body, his dream mind, and his dream soul.

From the shadows in the eyes of those around him came strange signals to his brain. There was something not quite right about the way they acted. In fact, a few of them he knew were dead, and most of the rest were much older than what they appeared to be now.

Oliver felt a bizarre correlation forming in his mind.

Yes, his mind.

This was in his mind.

Everything was within himself.

Was he asleep?

Holy shit, he was asleep.

Holy fucking shit, he was dreaming.

But, a dream?

He was awake?

How could that be?

Oliver tried to comprehend what was going on. He strained to see the image that was buried far inside himself. But how could he look at something without the eyes to see it or even the it to be seen? He didn't have time to accept what was happening. Mindlessness was pulling him back in. His thoughts began to drift into another dream. He forced himself to focus in order to stay aware of where he was.

The hazy blue sky.

The shadowy faces he knew so well.

Golden buildings that sat in strange angles all around him.

He was in prefect clarity, and everything was more real than reality itself. The most stunning aspect of his dream world was the distant horizon of purple mountains, which he perceived more vividly than anything else. In truth, they were nothing more than his own imagination, but to him his imagination was absolute beauty.

Upwards, Oliver thought, was where he ought go. Flying was his only desire. He lifted himself up, or rather pushed everything else down, and he was surprised to see that he did this act with ease. The universe was moving to his every whim because the entire universe was his very mind.

It was then that Oliver's excitement betrayed him, awakening his body to a dull and familiar reality. His bedroom was aglow with the early morning sunrise. His skin was warm beneath the large blue covers of his bed. His shoulder, however, had escaped the blankets and sat in the open cool air.

Oliver lay there, recalling his dream. He pulled the warm blankets over his body and remembered the awareness of being within himself. He could still see the details that were born within his mind, and he could remember well the clarity that he had possessed when he looked deep into his being. What most distinctly remained, however, was the lingering emotion that he had felt within the dream. It still sat heavy within his heart, and he couldn't quite define what it was.

Slowly the day ahead took over his thoughts. It was Christmas Eve, and he would later be with his family. Good appearances would have to be put on. He had to be Oliver Radcliff.

But what about his lucid dream? It was unlike anything he had ever experienced before. Though now he couldn't quite remember how it happened. In fact, he couldn't really remember much about it at all. Other than that he knew it had occurred, nothing seemed to remain within his head. Just a few minutes ago it was fresh within his mind, yet as he tried and tried to recollect what he experienced, nothing would return. Even the peculiar emotion that he had felt was gone without a trace.

Oliver gave a heavy sigh as he rolled out of bed. He walked to his bedroom window and spread open the blinds with his hand. The sky was bright and blue. Snow had fallen through the night and covered the world below. The street beside his apartment was well plowed, however, and it gleamed a wet black contrast against the bright landscape surrounding it.

Oliver let his hand go from the blinds, and the thin plastic blades flimsily snapped shut. He wandered his way into the bathroom, where he slowly brushed his teeth and gazed at his reflection. It was then that a fraction of his dream returned. He remembered seeing the mountains in the distance and nothing else.

What were they?

And what did they represent?

And then he remembered something else. It was the sensation he felt when he became awake within his dream. It was complete wonder, and it was something he hadn't known for a very long time.

Oliver spat a foamy mouthful of toothpaste into the sink. He then washed away the rest with swigs of water. Walking back into his bedroom, he slipped off his clothes.

There he stood staring at his naked body in the mirror. He was a pale white human and awkwardly long-limbed. The hair on his legs was much thicker than that which grew on the rest of his body. His penis hung there like any other man's. His balls were somewhat uneven, with one side being larger and lower than the other. He was thin and could make out the shape of his ribs pushing against the skin of his chest. His waist gently curved inward, giving him a slightly feminine shape. He did note, however, that though he was rather skinny he possessed a faintly muscular physique. It was as if his body had the potential to be some animalistic warrior but was instead trapped in a world that turned him into sad putty.

Oliver lifted his arm and flexed it in front of his chest.

Nothing much there.

He finished getting dressed and stumbled to the kitchen. There he made a bowl of cereal and ate it standing beside the fridge. A moment later he sat upon the floor of his front room, wrapping the Christmas presents he got for everyone.

There was a journal for Claire, which had a red cloth cover and gilded pages. Each day presented a question to ask yourself about life. Oliver thought it might help her figure out a few things. He knew that being a teenager was a strange time full of questions and that finding out who you were was the hardest one of all.

For his youngest sister Faye, Oliver had built a homemade planetarium that she could use in her room at night. With the help of Mike's electrical know-how, he had made it a few months back. It was a small black dodecahedron, which, as Oliver learned while making it, was a word that stood for something that had twelve sides. Within it was an array of lights that Mike had put together. Its surface was pierced with a myriad of holes, which would let the light shine through upon Faye's walls. Oliver hoped she would like it. She always seemed to him to be a little too down to Earth for a child. He thought that giving her something to look up at would point her head to the sky.

Oliver always had trouble figuring out what to get his father, and he forever ended up buying some sort of generic fatherly gift for him. A mug with footballs on it. Socks with Dad printed on the side. Or even a book about being a respectable man, which Oliver thought would connect a deeper part of himself with his father.

It didn't.

This year, though, he got something a little more sincere. It was an old tin motorcycle that had shown up at Ouro's one day. Along with it came a book on the history of motorbikes, which Oliver gave to Claire to give to their father. After looking up how much the little worn-out motorcycle was worth, which was at least a hundred bucks, he talked the owner of the store into selling it to him for much less. They had gotten it for free, even though they shouldn't have, because someone thought they were a charity like Salvation Army or something. The owner agreed to sell it to him, and Oliver eagerly bought it, anticipating that it would be the first gift for his father that actually meant something.

As for Jeanne, Oliver bought her a set of floral scented candles. He didn't really know her well enough to buy her something special, even though he had begun to slowly grow close to her. He had learned through life, however, that there were certain things you could buy women that they would always seem to like. Candles were one of them, so he bought some for Jeanne.

Lastly, he wrapped the painting he was giving to Mike and Michelle and Audrey. It was of the photo Michelle took in India of the river Ganges, though he had tainted it with his messy, expressive touch.

Oliver checked the time, realizing he had better leave if he wanted to make it to his family's house for lunch. He gathered up all the presents he had wrapped, and he put them in a white trash bag.

He felt foolishly like Santa Claus as he put on his coat and tossed the bag over his shoulder. As he left his apartment and began to walk down the snow-covered sidewalk, he imagined himself as a parent playing the fatherly role of a Santa. The idea of it actually brought him a hint of happiness, but then he quickly questioned why.

Did he want to be a father?

Did he want to raise another living being?

And his desires aside, would he ever really be one?

He hadn't been in a relationship for years. Though he did enjoy being alone, he couldn't deny the fact that he wanted somebody to be close to. He longed for that intimate ambition which everyone felt when they were with someone new. It was like the world was reborn. It was pure youth.

But Oliver knew that every mirage would eventually fade, and that behind it all hid the same old life.

No, that wasn't true.

Life changes every time we interact with another.

So being in love with someone, even though it may come to a dead end, changes who we are.

Maybe that was the transformation he needed?

Maybe he wanted love to push him forward?

Perhaps even a family would do him good. He could have a child and forget all about his own desires. He could take it upon himself to care for his family and nothing more.

But that was a skewed and inexperienced view upon parenthood. He knew that he was just rambling on in his head for reasons unknown. The simple fact of the matter was that he would enjoy having a woman in his life, whether it lasted or not, and that someday he would probably like to settle down and have a family. For now though, he had too much to take care of inside of himself before he could start giving his all to another.

Oliver had made it to Mike's house, realizing that the entire walk there was spent inside his head. He stopped to look around at the brightly shining winter day. He noticed the sharp, gray bark on the trees, the rows of similar houses that lined both sides of the street, and the infinite shimmer of the snowflakes lying smoothly against the ground. He turned his head upwards, gazing at the vibrant blue sky. He closed his eyes and listened to the sound of nearly nothing entering his senses. The quite drone of cars in the distance and the wavering gusts of wind were the only sounds that met him.

He then tried to smell the world, but the cold December air didn't carry much of an aroma. He refused to believe that there was nothing there to smell, however, and continued to breathe with intensity the empty winter air.

"Oliver?" Michelle asked from a short distance away.

He opened his eyes and turned to see her standing in the doorway of her house. She was smiling. Beside her stood Audrey with eyes gazing wide at him.

"Oh," he stuttered quietly to himself, walking through the snow-covered lawn. He smiled back as he stepped onto their front porch. "I was just taking things in." He paused to rub away the snot that was forming along the bottom of his nose. "Well, really, I was coming by to see you guys for a moment, and then I got sidetracked when I stopped to take it all in."

"Oh yeah?" she asked. "And what was it that you found?"

"Lots, I guess," he answered, rubbing his nose. "The world and such." He looked around again at the landscape he had just been aware of. "But I couldn't seem to smell anything. I guess snow just doesn't have a scent."

"It does too," Michelle replied.

"Oh, really?" Oliver asked. "What is it like?"

"It's like snow," she answered, grinning. "You probably just can't smell it because you're freezing to death." She waved at him to come inside as she opened the door wide. "Get in here."

He stomped his shoes over and over again on the concrete patio, watching as the snow fell off in clumps, and then walked into the front entryway of their house.

"Hello," Audrey said to him timidly.

"Hello," he said back with a smile.

"Merry Christmas!" she suddenly yelled.

"Well, Merry Christmas to you too," he told her, setting his bag of gifts onto the floor. Audrey walked up to it and poked the side with her finger.

"Whatcha got?" Michelle asked, nodding her head.

"Presents, of course," he replied. "Where's Mike?"

"Right here," Mike answered, walking into the entryway.

"Hello!" Oliver said joyfully, which was atypical of him. "And Merry Christmas!"

"Same to you, man. Same to you," Mike said with a smile. He was drinking a cup of coffee and was still in his light green pajamas.

"Can't stay long," Oliver told them, "but I've got a gift for you guys." He reached down into his bag and pulled out a shoddily wrapped present.

"Can I open it?" Audrey asked loudly, pulling at Michelle's pant leg.

"Well, is it for you?" her mother asked back.

"It is," Oliver cut in. "It's for all of you. But be careful opening it. Might be a bit fragile."

"Go ahead," Michelle said to her daughter.

Audrey slowly inched forward to Oliver. He handed her the large, flat, rectangular gift. She awkwardly held it with her arms spread wide, sitting down where she stood and tearing apart the wrapping paper.

"It's a painting!" the three-year-old shouted.

"You said it would look nice outside her room," Oliver said, rubbing the back of his head.

"It's amazing!" Michelle said, leaning down to gaze at it.

"What is it?" Audrey asked.

"It's a far away place your dad and I went to a long time ago," Michelle answered her daughter. She caressed her hand along the painting's edge. "It's really beautiful, Oliver."

"Really beautiful!" Audrey shouted out.

"Thanks," he replied.

"What do you say to Oliver?" Michelle asked Audrey.

"Thank you," she said in a long, drawn out tone.

"You're welcome," he said, almost bowing.

"Here you go," Mike said, walking back into the hallway and handing a gift to Oliver.

Oliver hadn't even noticed that Mike had left.

"Oh, thanks," Oliver said, taking the gift.

"Don't open it now," Mike told him. "Do it when you're bored and lonely. It'll be good then."

"Well, hey, I'm bored and lonely most of the time," Oliver joked, though with a slight sense of sincerity. He placed the gift in his bag and lifted the bag over his shoulder.

"Whoa, nice painting," Mike said, seeing it for the first time. "You did that?"

"I did," Oliver replied. "It's for you guys."

"Thanks, man," Mike said, leaning down beside his wife and daughter. "It's really good. Really good."

"Thanks," Oliver said, adjusting the bag upon his shoulders.

"So you're going to your family's?" Mike asked, standing up.

"Yup," Oliver replied. "In fact, I need to get going."

"It was nice seeing you, Oliver," Michelle said, standing and stepping closer to him. She gave him a gentle hug, and he smiled.

"It was," Mike added. "Make sure to tell your family we said hello."

"I will," Oliver replied, turning to the door.

"Thanks again for the painting," Michelle said. "It's amazing."

"Merry Christmas!" Audrey yelled out.

"Merry Christmas," Oliver said, leaving them and returning to the bright outdoors. As he walked alone to his family's house, he wondered whether or not his painting was actually good. Did his friends really like it, or were they just being kind?

Could something really be good anyway? Good and bad are just an opinion. The value of anything is up to anyone. And if that's true, then the only proper thing for him to do was make what he himself thought was good.

That's when something clicked inside of him.

It was the realization that he should be himself, that he would inevitably be himself, and that he couldn't be anything else but himself. There was nothing to do besides live, and with that understanding came complete wonder at his existence. In a way, the world before him wasn't any different from his dream. It was simply nothing being something.

Or perhaps it was the other way around.

Either way, it was this.

Forget success. Oliver had a new goal in mind.

It was to awaken to this dream.

To awaken to his life.

Decorticated
Or, Without Is Now Within

Claire felt every warm droplet of water against her skin. Each one collided with her senses, caressing down her body and reminding her of the way she felt last night.

Or rather, the way that he felt her.

Claire's eyes were closed. She was motionless, slowly breathing in the moist air that filled the shower. Her body was entirely new, as if today was the first day she had ever lived within it. Her hands and fingers and feet and toes, her arms and legs and shoulders and hips, her eyes and mouth and ears and nose, her breasts and her vagina. Every part of her was born right then and there in the small bathroom of her family's house on the morning of Christmas Eve.

Though her body was new, Claire's mind was the same stream of thoughts as before. That's not to say that it hadn't changed. Rather, instead of being born again, her mind had merely altered its course. Transformed from experience, her thoughts flowed down a more authentic path. It was a passage known by many, yet only by those who had learned to live.

Memories of the night before arose within Claire.

Driving through the cold darkness, Joel sat quietly beside her. Then, into the warm lights of someone's house, they found both friends and strangers.

Talking and laughing and yelling.

Drinks and more drinks.

Just one for her and him, however.

Or maybe two.

Or three.

They escaped the noise and the lights, and they found each other in the dark. In a lightless room they spoke of life and what it meant to them. They talked of who they were and who they wanted to be. Then they spoke in heavy silence, touching lips, hands, and bodies.

He wasn't the first to know her skin, her lips, her hidden inner places, but he was the only one that had ever awoken her to life. She would still be a virgin after that night, but she would no longer be a sleeping child. She was a woman, and she was wide-awake.

Claire and Joel left the party early. The buzz they had gotten from their few drinks had been quickly burnt away in the desire of each other's bodies. Claire sat in the passenger seat of Joel's car as they drove home through the cold night. She watched the snowflakes flying by like stars in their headlights.

The two of them talked of how they would never see each other again, and though it ought to have been a sad conversation, it wasn't. Neither of them wanted the other for any longer than they already had. All they really needed was that single night of transformation together.

Claire did feel a certain emotion as he drove away, though she didn't think of it as love or longing. To her, it was merely peace.

She let Joel slip out of her mind. He wasn't a part of who she had become. He was a place in her past and nothing more. The water that ran across her body began to lose its warmth, so she turned off the shower and pushed aside the curtain. She reached for her towel, which hung nearby, and dried herself off before the cold air could take over the room and chill her skin.

With a towel wrapped around her body, Claire stood before the foggy mirror. She wiped away the steam that had collected upon its surface. Within the clarity that was left behind, she saw an eighteen-year-old woman who knew entirely everything and absolutely nothing.

"What now?" she asked herself, leaning closer to the mirror and staring deep into her reflection. It became foggy again as she waited for an answer. She accepted the opaqueness of life's reply and knew that she would never really know what to do, which meant that the only thing she could do was live her life as it was in every present moment.

Claire opened the bathroom door and hurriedly walked to her bedroom, which was barren compared to what it used to be. Most of her belongings were inside the large cardboard box sitting in her closet.

She grabbed the clothes she needed, glimpsing the cardboard box as it sat at her feet. She turned away and got dressed, leaving her hair hanging wet against her back. A distant memory of her mother suddenly appeared. She wasn't sure what had brought it forth. In fact, it was a rather insignificant memory. The two of them were standing in line at a department store. Claire was six or seven years old. She was watching her mother talk to the cashier about the price of something or other. The words being spoken weren't memorable. It was the expression on her mother's face that remained. She looked so intent in her ways, so mature and strong.

Claire sat on the edge of her bed, letting the memory occupy her thoughts until it quietly faded away. Her brand new body and altered state of mind were feeling impressions of a distant sadness, but Claire refused to let it come any closer. Her life had to move forward, which meant she had to leave her past behind.

She left her room and made her way downstairs. In the living room she met Jeanne sitting alone upon the sofa. She was drinking a cup of tea and reading a magazine about cooking.

"Dad and Faye still gone?" Claire asked, sitting down in the chair across from Jeanne.

"Yeah," she replied, closing the magazine and setting it beside her. "They're picking up some food after they drop off Faye's friend."

"What kind?" Claire asked.

"Chinese, I think," she answered.

"Sounds good," Claire said, running a hand through her cold, damp hair. "Nothing like lo mein on Christmas Eve."

"I can't believe it's Christmas again," Jeanne said with a melancholy face. "Time is moving fast. Really fast. I'm gonna be eighty before I know it."

"Yeah, and I'll be your age," Claire joked, in the hope it would lighten Jeanne's mood.

"This would have been," Jeanne replied, ending her sentence short and pausing for a moment to think. "This would have been his twenty-third Christmas. My son that is."

"Corey, right?" Claire asked sympathetically, to which Jeanne silently nodded yes.

"Life is damn hard," she said, looking to Claire. "But it keeps on going no matter what, so there's no reason to let it keep on digging you down. We don't have a choice but to go forward, and that's what makes everything all right, I suppose."

"Easier said than done," Claire said.

"That's true, but that shouldn't stop someone from trying."

"You're right. But what if they can't go on?

"Everyone can. No matter how hard it may seem."

"You just have to be yourself, I guess," Claire said, standing.

"Mhmm," Jeanne hummed, returning to her magazine.

Just then the door opened. Oliver walked in looking slightly different than he usually did. He wasn't smiling, but his body carried itself in a lighter manner.

"Hello," he said, turning and waving to them. He sat a large bag on the floor beside him and began to take off his coat.

"Hi, Oliver," Jeanne said, standing.

"Hello," Claire followed.

"Where's Dad?" he asked, walking into the room.

"Out with Faye to get food," Jeanne told him.

"I'll be right back," Claire said, walking by Oliver. As she passed him she gently sat her hand on his shoulder.

She walked up the stairs to her room, where she finished getting ready for the day. Her life was vibrantly happening right before her eyes, and for the first time in a long time she felt she belonged within the person named Claire.

Your Magnificent Fate
Or, The Life And Death Of Everything

Christmas commercials played on the television screen. Imaginary families bundled up in nice clothing made jokes about their distraught imaginary lives. The punch line of it all was how everything would better if they just had new things.

Faye sat alone in the living room, not watching the TV but hearing its noise. Her eyes were instead set upon the window across the room. On the other side of it the sun was setting, and the fading sky burned with vivid color. As she stared out of the window, she wondered about life. She did so in the way a young child would, with thoughts that were innocent and confused. Within them, though, she was discovering the seed of wisdom

"No way," Claire said, walking into the room. "Green tea is way better than coffee."

"Tea is good," Oliver said, following her, "but coffee has that burntness to it that I love."

"Eh, it's alright," Claire replied. "It kinda upsets my stomach. But tea tastes great and makes me feel good too."

"Well," Oliver said, falling down upon the sofa beside Faye, "why don't we ask Faye?"

He looked to her, and she looked up to him.

"Apple juice," she answered, smiling. "I haven't had coffee. And tea isn't that great. But apple juice is the best."

"There you have it," Claire said, falling into the nearby chair. She raised her legs and placed them upon the coffee table.

"What's on?" Oliver asked Faye.

"*How the Grinch Stole Christmas*," she answered.

"Oh," he replied. "Mom used to love this one."

Just then the commercials ended and the television screen was filled with a bright blue cartoon sky. There was a silence amongst the three siblings as they watched.

Faye, though staring at the TV, was deeper in thought than she was before. She was sent there by her brother's words. She thought about her mom and how she had died a long time ago. Faye had always sort of known this, but never really thought about it. It was just a hazy fact that drifted through her life, never amounting to much more than a passing curiosity in who her mother was.

Faye had never really understood what it meant that her mother had died. She had never known her, so it was hard for her to acknowledge that she was alive in the first place. But at this moment she was connecting ideas within her mind, grasping new facets of a reality that she was growing into every day.

Her mother was dead. This meant that at one point she was alive. Someone couldn't die unless they were alive. Faye realized that her mother had been a living, breathing person just like her, and when she passed away she must have gone to wherever it was that people went when they died.

If her mom was there, then what did Faye have to fear? No matter where she ended up after life, her mother would find her.

Faye snapped away from her thoughts. She was back within the living room, taking in the images and sounds that poured into her senses. The TV was again overtaken by commercials. Claire reached for the remote control and muted the television.

"I can't stand commercials," she said.

"What was Mom like?" Faye asked.

There was a pause.

"She was beautiful," Claire said after a moment.

Oliver nodded in agreement.

"She was kind and funny and smart," he said. "Nobody could make you feel the way she did. It was as if everything was okay when she was there, no matter what."

"She sounds nice," Faye said, staring at the silent TV screen. A commercial for toothpaste was playing. A large pair of smiling lips, with glistening white teeth, was snowboarding over mountains of peppermint toothpaste. Faye turned to Oliver. "What do you think happened to her when she died?"

"Well," he slowly said, though no explanation followed.

Claire stood from her seat and walked out of the room. Oliver glanced at her as she did, and Faye thought he had a strange look on his face.

"I know I'm young," Faye said, "but I'm getting older. I understand that things die. I've been thinking about it a lot lately. Do you ever think about dying?"

"I do," he answered, rubbing his hair. "I think everyone does. It's a pretty big part of life."

"Does it ever scare you?" she asked.

"It scares me a lot." he replied. "Does it scare you?"

Faye quickly nodded yes.

"Well, you're not alone," he said. "Mostly everyone is scared of dying. But even though we're scared of death it doesn't make it bad. We're just scared of it because we don't know what it is. For all we know, dying could be a beautiful thing."

"I read about dying," she said, "and reencarnshun."

"You mean reincarnation?" he asked, smiling.

"Yeah, that. I read about it, and what life and death are too"

"Where did you read that?"

"In a book from the library."

"So what do you think life and death are?"

Faye tilted her head and hummed to herself, thinking of her answer and trying to find a way to say it.

"I think life is feeling things," she said, "and death is not feeling things."

"That's probably the best answer anyone's ever had," he said, setting his hand on her shoulder.

"But I don't like to think about not feeling anything," she said.

"Yeah, that can be scary," he told her. "Feeling things is what makes us who we are. So not feeling anything would make us no one, huh? But who's to say we can't feel something again? Maybe we could be someone brand new? And if that's true, then were we really the old person in the first place? Or were we just the feeling?"

"Uhm," Faye stuttered, confused. "I dunno."

"Here," Claire said from behind them, walking back into the room. She sat upon the arm of the sofa. In her hands was a small black and white photograph of a lady Faye didn't recognize. "That's Mom," Claire said, handing the picture to Faye, "when she was young."

"She's pretty," Faye said. She really did think so.

"Mia Simon was her name," Claire said, "before she married Dad. Then she became Mia Radcliff."

"Faye and I were just talking about life and death," Oliver said.

"Oh, really?" Claire replied.

"What do you think about it?" Faye asked her sister.

"Well, I dunno." she replied. "I think dying is scary."

"So do we," Faye agreed.

"But death is a part of life," Claire continued, "and there's no point in being afraid of what's going to happen no matter what."

"Do you think Mom was afraid when she died?" Faye asked. At this, she saw a change in Claire's face. She knew that her sister was sad, and she regretted asking the question. She watched as a tear fell down from Claire's eye.

"I think that in the end everyone feels okay," Oliver said. Faye turned to him as he continued to talk. "Dying might hurt, but being dead probably isn't so bad."

"It's the goodbye that really hurts," Claire said, rubbing her cheek and sniffling. "After Mom died we were still alive. We had to live without her. It was hard, and it still is. I imagine she felt the same way when she left us. The goodbye hurts a lot."

"But maybe there's a hello after that," Faye said, feeling bad for her sister. She nearly began to cry herself as she spoke. "It's called reencarnshun." She said the word purposely wrong in the hope it would make her sister smile, which it did.

"Hey, it's Christmas Eve," Oliver said, standing, "So let's enjoy being alive. Okay?"

"Yes, let's," Claire said, rubbing the last of her tears away.

"Christmas!" Faye yelled out, smiling. "Where's Dad?"

"He's upstairs with Jeanne," Claire said. "I'll go get them. We should all do something together."

As Claire walked away, Oliver stood beside his little sister and looked to her.

"You okay?" he asked.

"Yup," Faye answered, thinking to herself about Christmas.

Her fears melted away as the warmth of her imagination crept into her head. She pictured tomorrow morning, which would bring a living room full of presents from Santa.

But, she wondered, wouldn't Santa die someday too?

If everyone has to, then why wouldn't he?

She pushed the question away, embracing a newfound wisdom within herself, one which, unbeknownst to her, was wise beyond her years. Yes, Santa would someday die, but for now he was alive, so there was no point in worrying about the future. She should instead learn to love everything that was going on right now, since that's really all there ever was.

December 25th, 2013
Or, A String Of Lights

Color played across Arthur's eyes.

Sounds danced within his ears.

This was a moment much like any other, yet it was nonetheless a moment eternally unique. Never before and never again would the universe exist as it was, yet it would always seem to be somewhat the same. Arthur's life was floating before him at a distance neither far nor close. His ego wasn't to be found, but its imprint remained.

He was who he was without being himself.

Snow fell slow and heavy outside the kitchen window. Arthur stared at every frozen particle as it drifted past the colored lights that hung from his house. In his right hand was a half empty glass of red wine. In his left was nothing.

Soft footsteps drew near until they came to a stop. Arthur turned to see Jeanne standing beside him. She smiled.

"Hello," he said, wading closer through the cosmos to the world that was his normal life.

"Hello," she replied, wrapping her arms around him. "Faye's ready for bed. She wants to talk to you."

"I'd love to talk to her too," he said, taking a drink from his wine. His lips moved to Jeanne's cheek, where they pressed softly against her skin, leaving behind a nearly inexistent remainder of fermented grapes. She let him go as he stepped away.

Arthur walked to the stairway, feeling his life drift apart yet again. As he climbed each of the steps that led upstairs, however, he felt it return with a heavy thud. When he glimpsed Faye's brightly lit bedroom door ajar he snapped completely into place within himself.

He was Arthur. He was a father. He was human.

His daughter smiled as he walked into her room. She was lying above the covers of her bed and holding a book in her hands. It was a gift she had gotten from Santa.

"Reading your book?" he asked, sitting down beside her.

"Yup," she replied, turning the pages. "I like it a lot." She looked up to him and tilted her head. "Did you know that we're made of the same things that stars are?"

"I did," he answered, brushing his hand across her hair. "The whole universe is pretty much made of the same thing. Everything is just this one something, only that it's put together in different ways and places and times."

Faye's eyes looked to him as if she couldn't comprehend what he had said, yet her lips slightly curled up into an open smile, revealing a hint of understanding within, or at least amusement.

"Did you have a good Christmas?" he asked. She nodded yes and looked back down to her book.

"I'm kinda sad it's over," she said.

"Yeah, that's what happens," he told her. "The good times go by fast. But there's always next Christmas. And besides, you don't have to go to school for another week. I wish I had that much time off."

"Does life go fast?" Faye asked, still looking down at her book.

"What do you mean, sweetie?" he replied.

"Does life go by fast?" she asked again, this time looking up to him. "Someday I'll be old like you. And you used to be young like me. Did it take a long time to get old?"

"Well," Arthur paused, realizing he had to actually think about his answer. After a moment of silence he continued. "Yes, it did take a long time. It took a really long time. But when you look back on the past it seems as if it took no time at all."

"So yes and no?" she interrupted.

"Yes and no," he agreed, nodding his head and grinning.

"Everything is yes and no," she said slightly bothered. "I don't think anyone knows anything."

"You're probably right," Arthur told her, placing his hand upon her back. "And you're one amazing girl to know this. Most people live their whole lives thinking they know everything, or at least thinking that someone else does. That's when bad things happen."

"Why?"

"Because people will do anything, bad or good, when they think they're right."

"So I shouldn't ever think I'm right?"

"It's not that you shouldn't believe in yourself. You just need to be open to the idea that you might just be wrong. Only when someone admits that they don't know can they really find the answer."

"Well, what's the answer then?"

"I don't know," Arthur said with a smile.

"That doesn't help me much," Faye replied, closing her book and crawling up to the top of her bed.

"I'm sorry, babe," Arthur said, pulling the blankets up and over his daughter. "But you don't have much to worry about. You've got a long, long life ahead of you to think about it. For now it's bedtime. You've got quite a day tomorrow, doing whatever you want to do, so cherish being seven years old."

"I'm scared of dying," she said with faint tears in her eyes.

"Oh, honey," Arthur said, sitting close beside her and gently placing his hand upon her face. "You don't need to be afraid of that. I know it's scary, but you don't need to think about it. You've got so much life ahead, and I swear I won't let anything happen to you."

"I'm trying not to be scared," she coughed out between dry sobs, "I know I'm alive and okay. But someday I'll die, even if I do live a long time."

"That's true. I won't lie to you about that, even if it would make you feel better. But you have to trust me when I say that you don't need to worry about it. As you get older you'll understand more. It might not be easy, and you might even understand less before you do, but someday you'll get closer to knowing the answer. You'll be able to look at life and death without being afraid."

"Like you? Are you afraid?"

"I'm not afraid, no. I used to be. When your mother passed away, dying was all I could think about. But lately I've started to be brave. And when you're brave you can see that there's really nothing to be afraid of at all."

"Why?"

"Because we're made of the same things that stars are made of. Because we'll always be here, and we'll someday be stars again. Because if you're you and you're brave and you do what you think is right, then what have you got to lose?"

"Hey, I knew that," Faye said, sniffling.

"See, look at how close you already are to knowing," Arthur said, brushing her hair away from her face. "So just be brave for me, okay? Promise?"

"But I can't ever know, remember? If I think I know then I'm wrong, right?"

"First off, you're too smart for your age. And secondly, maybe I was wrong. Maybe you can know the truth. After all, I couldn't be right, because then I'd be wrong."

"What?"

"Exactly."

"You're making fun of me!" Faye laughed. "I'm confused."

"That's because I love you," he said, bending over and kissing her cheek. "Now, two things. One, will you be brave for me?"

"Yeah," she answered, slowly nodding with a half-smile.

"And two, will you go to sleep?"

"No!" she yelled out, her smile growing into fullness.

"Goodnight, Faye," Arthur said, ignoring her answer and standing. She replied by sticking her tongue out at him. "I love you," he said back.

"I love you too, Dad," she said, pointing to her nightlight beside the door. Arthur bent over and switched it on before stepping out of the room. He stood in the hallway, preparing himself to walk right back in as soon as he heard his daughter not attempting to sleep. But after a moment, no sounds followed, so he walked to the stairs at the end of the hallway.

The second floor of Arthur's house was always warmer than that of the first, and as he reached the middle steps of the stairway, he closed his eyes and slowed to a stop so that he could feel the changing air against his skin. It was subtle, but it was a difference that he could always sense.

"Dad?" he heard Claire say, awakening him from his slow motion. "You okay?"

"Oh, yeah," he replied. "Just being my weird self."

"Yeah, I'd say so," she said back, standing at the bottom of the stairs. She walked up a few of the steps. "It was a good Christmas, don't ya think?"

"It was," he answered. "I love having the time to be with you kids. And thanks again for the book. It's wonderful."

"No problem. You're my dad and all, so I gotta get you something good. You should thank Oliver though. He was the one who found it."

"Speaking of, where is he?"

"I think he's outside, smoking."

"Really?"

"Why else would he be outside," she answered, slightly laughing. "But I dunno. He might not be."

"For the love of hell, please don't take up smoking, Claire."

"Meh," she answered, waving her hand. "I don't like the smell, so I don't think you have much to worry about."

"That's good," he replied, not knowing what else to say. The two of them stood awkwardly quiet until Claire continued to walk her way up the stairs. "Going to bed?" Arthur asked.

"Kinda," Claire answered. "I'm just gonna think for a while."

"You know, I'm proud to have you as my daughter, Claire," Arthur said, stepping aside and leaning against the railing. "This is certainly an oversimplification, but it seems to me that not many teenagers stop to just think these days. And not to sound conceited either, but you remind me of myself when I was your age."

"I'm pretty sure you just said two of the most stereotypical dad things to say," she laughed.

"Well, I am a dad through and through. But I wasn't always one, you know. From one human being to another, you're an amazing person, Claire Radcliff. Your mother would have been proud."

A bittersweet happiness came upon Claire's face. She quickly stepped forward and hugged Arthur. He squeezed her tight, and for a brief moment he felt as if he was hugging a sort of echo of Mia. In his arms was his beautiful daughter, a living breathing human being whose inner and outer self was shaped by the very essence that was his wife.

"Thank you for saying so. It means a lot, Dad," she said, letting go of him. "But I'm really not that great, and I'm alright with that. I'd rather be myself than amazing, even if it meant that I was just a useless lump of teenager."

"Oh, come on, Claire."

"I'm not saying that's what I am!" she said, walking backwards up the steps. "I'm just saying that I'd rather be myself than anything else. I know that I'm not useless or a waste or whatever negative things I could call myself. In fact, I think I've finally found what I'm good at."

"And what's that?" Arthur asked.

"I'm really quite good at living," she answered as she reached the top of the steps.

"That's the best thing there is to be good at," he replied.

"Good night, Dad," she said with a wave of her hand. "Love you."

"Love you too, Claire," he said, watching her walk away.

Arthur finally reached the bottom of the steps, where he paused to let his life flow easily by. After a minute or so of this half-meditation, he walked to the kitchen. There, he stood with his half-empty glass of wine again in his hand. Looking back into the multicolored glow outside the window, he downed the rest of his drink and forced his awareness upon the delicate burn that drizzled down his throat.

He wondered where Jeanne was, but soon discovered that she was asleep upon the family room sofa. Standing beside her, he glimpsed through the front window the movement of his son. He quietly walked to the door and opened it.

Standing on the edge of the porch was Oliver staring out into the lazily falling snow. Arthur quickly noticed that there was no cigarette in his hand, but he felt the need to test his son nonetheless.

"Having a smoke?" he asked.

"No, actually," Oliver replied. "I'm just thinking."

"Good," Arthur said, walking closer.

"But what if I was?" Oliver asked with a mischievous eye.

"Then I'd slap it right out of your hands."

"No, you wouldn't."

"I know. But I am your father, and I do have to tell you what to do sometimes. It's your choice though. You can do whatever you want. Hell, I used to smoke. And hell, so did lots of great people. But still, you shouldn't smoke."

"Well, I ran out a couple days ago anyway," Oliver said, sticking his hands into his pockets, "and I haven't bought any since. I'm trying to be better to myself. I'm tired of being some sad, tortured, genius artist sort of thing."

"That's good," Arthur replied. "You never were much of a genius."

"Thanks," Oliver said, kicking a small bit of snow at his feet.

"I'm joking, Oliver."

"I know."

"So if you're not a depressed artist, then who are you?"

Oliver didn't answer. He just stared out into the snow. A moment later, however, he suddenly turned and faced his father.

"No one," he answered.

"Lucky you," Arthur said.

"Yeah, I know," he replied, smiling.

Arthur hadn't seen his son smile so genuinely in a long time.

Seeing it made him return a smile just as sincere.

"So what are you gonna do with your life?" he asked.

"I'm still gonna paint," Oliver replied. "I think I'll be even better at it, really. I'm not gonna try anymore."

"That doesn't sound too productive."

"Sure it is," Oliver said. "When you're no one, trying just gets in the way."

"Well put, I suppose," Arthur said.

"Eh, it's all just words. What I really mean can only be experienced, you know? But look at me, sounding like some sort of enlightened sage. I don't really know anything. I guess I'm just accepting that I don't know."

"Funny," Arthur said, "your little sister and I just talked about the same thing. Us Radcliffs are awfully strange."

"Nah," Oliver replied, "we're just like everyone else."

"You're probably right."

"You do have to wonder though."

"Wonder what?" Arthur asked.

"What's it like to be someone else?" Oliver replied.

"You can never know," Arthur said.

"Because if you were someone else then you wouldn't be you."

"Exactly."

"I think we just discovered eternal life," Oliver said, grinning.

"What? Why?" Arthur asked back.

"If you're always you no matter who you are, then you'll always be alive, even if you're not the you who you thought you were before."

"I get you. But maybe I don't. Too many words."

"Yeah, that happens."

"Hey, thanks again for the little old motorcycle," Arthur said, patting his son on the shoulder. "I love it."

"I thought you would," Oliver said, nodding his head.

"I can't believe Christmas has come and gone again."

"That's life. It flies by."

"Just wait until you're in your fifties."

"I can only imagine."

"Some days I wake up and can't believe I'm as old as I am," Arthur said, walking to the other side of the porch. "Not that I'm really that old, but to think of all the days and nights and memories and forgotten moments in my life is baffling."

"Speaking of waking up," Oliver said, following Arthur to the other side of the porch, "or sleeping, rather. I had a lucid dream a few nights ago."

"Oh, really?" Arthur asked. He had always thought dreams were fascinating, especially lucid ones. His last book was even about them. It hadn't sold well, but to him it was the best thing he had ever written. "So you woke up within your dream? What was it like?"

"To be honest, I can't remember much," Oliver replied. "But I do know that it was amazing. There was so much emotion and creativity and meaning. If only real life were more like a dream, huh?"

"It is," Arthur said, brushing snow from the wooden railing beside him. "That's what many people lucid dream for, to see how our dreams aren't much different from our lives."

"Yeah, yeah. So life is an illusion. But what I meant was that I wish real life was a more exciting illusion."

"It's just the way you look it at, Oliver. Life can be amazing if you decide that it is."

"Yes, but I've decided that it's not. And that brings up a whole new problem for me."

"What's that?" Arthur asked.

"I can't believe that the universe comes down to this," Oliver answered, lightly gesturing to the world around them. "I want something fantastic, and I think existence would want that too. Why the hell are we living in a mundane world that runs on reason and logic and science?"

"Because that's just the way it is," Arthur told his son. "Like I said, it's all a matter of taste. You can decide to like this life or you can decide to hate it."

"But what if I want more than this life?" Oliver asked. "How do I decide whether to believe in myself or question myself? I could be moving towards something deeper or I could be getting lost in ignorance."

"That's a damn good question, and to tell the truth, I don't really know. I suppose it would be best to do both. Follow what you believe in, yet always question why you believe in it."

"Life is just too much," Oliver said, laughing without a smile.

"Well, it's no simple story," Arthur said, watching the snow falling before his eyes. "The plot's all over the place, but it never really goes anywhere. There's no point to much of anything. The beginning and end are kind of vague and nearly not even there. Loose ends lie everywhere, without any answers. Sometimes it can be exciting, but most of the time it's not. And, worst of all, the main character's confusing as hell."

"Sounds about right," Oliver said, standing beside his father.

"Eh, it's all just words," Arthur said, standing beside his son.